BEASTMODE

"Joe Awsum"

Published by:

G Street Chronicles
P.O. Box 490082
College Park, GA 30349

www.gstreetchronicles.com
Fan@gstreetchronicles.com

Editor: 21st Street Urban Editing & Publishing, LLC

Typesetting: G&S Typesetting & Ebook Conversion
info@gstypesetting.com

LCCN: 2010939157
ISBN: 978-0-9826543-9-2

Join us on Facebook G Street Chronicles Fan Page

Beastmode is dedicated to my father,
Gregory "Pops" Hasty
1954 - 2008

PART ONE

The Twins

December 25, 2001

The sixteen year old twins, Twon and Qwon, rose from their beds, anxious to see if their mom, who very rarely kept her word, just happened to keep it and got them those Jordan's they had been hounding her for. As they looked into the living room, two shoe boxes wrapped in newspaper sat under their tree, which was really a plant with some hand-made school ornaments on it they had made when they were younger. It was what it was in the projects. As they raced across the living room, damn near knocking over the coffee table that already had one leg held up by books, they wasted no time ripping in to the packages. Within seconds, they emerged with their Jordan's that they thought they would die without.

"Momma," the boys yelled simultaneously. There was no

response as they approached her bedroom door. The smell of stale Newports filled their nostrils as Qwon slowly pushed the door open with Twon right on his heels.

"Momma, you woke?" Twon said, pushing his brother aside.

There was no response from the motionless body in the bed. They continued to call out Momma as they made their way around the bed. They simultaneously noticed the belt tied around her arm tightly and just below, a needle hanging. "Momma," they yelled frantically as her eyes stared straight through them. Their attempts at reviving her failed. It couldn't be happening to them, not today. It really sank in quickly that the woman that gave birth to them was dead. Twon reached down slowly, closing his mother's eyes for the last time. Qwon then noticed a letter lying on the floor marked Twon and Qwon on it.

"Twins, I know right now you're confused and hurt, but it's important that you stay strong for each other. Always know I love y'all with all my heart and I will always be there, no matter where y'all go. Just know I couldn't go on a slave to this heroine any longer, and eventually my habit would become a liability to what the future holds for y'all. Now, this is where I need y'all to pay close attention. In the picture frame of y'all on my night stand, there is a key. This key is going to open a part of y'all life that can't be closed once it is opened—it is in your bloodline. Today is the ten year anniversary of the night those pussy ass police took your father away from us. Ten long years I've waited to give y'all this

key. The key to y'all's destiny, and now the time is here. I want y'all to go to our old house. It is boarded up now, but y'all will find a way in. Once inside, go up to your old room. Remember that mural of Michael Jordan y'all Dad had painted for y'all on the wall? It is time for y'all to find out the real reason it's there. Boys, there is one thing left...promise me you won't let those police ever take y'all away in handcuffs and lock y'all up, ever. Now go reclaim the throne your father left behind. You're the sons of King and boys, your father is waiting.

Love,
Mom.

P.S. I hope y'all like the shoes I got you for Christmas."

As they stood there trying to take in everything that had been put before them, strangely, they never shed a tear. It wasn't the first they had seen of death and it sure wouldn't be the last.

December 30, 2001

Social Services took no time stepping in and placing the twins in a group home. It was only temporary because it would only be a matter of time before they planned their escape. It was there mother's funeral, and the Social Worker took them and sat with them the entire time. As they sat in the church, they watched as hundreds of people made their way in and out, paying respect to Debra Scott, also known to the streets as Queen.

"Momma sure look good, huh, Qwon?"

"Sure do. She almost looks unreal," Qwon replied.

The years had taken a toll on Queen. Ten years ago, she was the baddest thing in the hood at one hundred-fifty pounds, with a five-three frame. Thick was an understatement. Her creamy black skin was complimented by her hypnotizing brown eyes that seemed to take complete control over their dad. He'd buy her the world if he could, and he sure did try. From minks, to diamonds, to clothes—you name it, she had it. Once their dad got locked up, it seemed like part of Queen died. The first couple of years were straight, but by the time they were nine, they noticed all her nice things their dad had bought her slowly disappeared. There were days at a time their momma wouldn't even come home, so they learned to take care of themselves. By their eleventh birthday, she had blown through a couple hundred thousand dollars that their dad had left her, and she was unable to continue paying the property taxes on their house. They were then forced to move to the Marion Jones housing projects. To some, it was unreal to hear Queen was living in the same projects her husband's legacy began in. At first, everything was going good. Momma walked around like the world was still hers. People jumped around doing whatever she asked, whenever she asked. As the months passed, Queen's ugly secret could no longer be hidden. Heroine called Queen night and day, and she answered. The people she once looked down upon, began to look down upon her as she'd sit on the stairway and nod off as the heroine stole her soul gram by gram. It was hard to believe the woman lying in the casket was once the Queen married to the infamous Tyler Scott, known to the twins as pops, but to the world as King.

As the door of the church opened, it was if nobody in the church was breathing. Mouths opened in awe as a massive six-four, two hundred ninety pounds of muscle walked in, shackled from waist to ankles, in a black suit. His braids were almost touching his chest and gold trims covering his devilish grin. His eyes were like heartless bullets spraying though the crowd, finally finding their targets; Twon and Qwon.

"Twon, it can't be," Qwon said, looking for the reassurance of his brother.

"Qwon, that's our dad."

It had been ten years since they'd seen their dad, and there he was shackled like an animal. To them, he was the most powerful and dangerous man in America. It wasn't always like that though.

As a young boy, Tyler Scott chased behind his two brothers through the slums of the city. It was hard on Grandma Scott raising three boys alone when death lied around every corner. As the boys got older, Grandma Scott could barely keep up with their mischief. If it wasn't one of them in trouble, it was all of them. Grandpa Scott had been killed a year after Tyler was born. The rumor was that Grandpa Scott robbed banks for a living, but the police could never prove it was him. The police caught him one night coming out of a bar and shot him down, making it look like a robbery gone bad. Grandma always told her boys, "Y'all gonna end up dead just like y'all daddy one day!" as if she were a scratched record. Soon, that song played its final tune.

"T", short for Terell, was always a ladies' man. He was

the oldest of the three brothers and at nineteen, he seemed to have every bitch in the city chasing his slim ass. That included the wife of the city's kingpin, Big Tony. Red was the quiet one of the brothers. He was two years younger than T and only a year older than Tyler. They constantly told T to leave Big Tony's wife alone, the whole hood knew what was going on and it was only a matter of time before Big Tony found out. But, there was no telling T shit, and he sure wasn't going to take the advice of his younger brothers.

One day in the projects, his luck ran out as he stood by their building trying to talk some girl out of her panties. He never heard death approaching in the form of Big Tony and his man, Slick. The girl's eyes grew big as if she'd seen a ghost over T's shoulder. T never got to turn around as gunfire ripped through the air. The first bullet exploded through the back of his skull, finding its way out his mouth, and barely missing the female, who was screaming. Blood and brain matter covered her face and clothes as T's body crumpled to the ground filled with fire. Twelve more bullets found their target as T's soul left his body. Big Tony added his final insult by pulling out his dick and pissing all over T's body and the female he was talking to. The police covered the projects everywhere asking questions. But, when it came to Big Tony, nobody would dare say anything in fear that their family would be next. Grandma Scott took it the worst. First her husband, now her son, it was just too much for her to bear. As Grandma watched the coroner put what was left of

T's bullet filled body in a bag, she collapsed from what later they found out was a massive heart attack and died on the scene only feet away from where her dead son once lay.

Red and Tyler stood there watching as the coroner took their older brother and their mother. To some it was strange that the surviving brothers never shed a tear.

Red just turned to his little brother and said, "You know what's gotta be done, right?"

"Yep," Tyler responded with no hesitation. It was at that very moment they both knew Big Tony had to die.

* * * * *

Big Tony never would have thought the two young assassins had been following his every move for two days. They were waiting in the shadows for the perfect moment to execute their plan. As Big Tony lay with his face deep in Peaches' pussy, the same pussy that two days ago got T killed, it would now be the same one that he was killed in.

"You know you are what you eat," Tyler said as he stood there with Red watching what was going on.

"What the fuck?" Big Tony said finally, coming up for air with his face dripping wet. "How the fuck did y'all get in here? Do you know what the fuck I am?" Big Tony questioned.

"Enough with the questions, we know exactly who you are. The fat bitch that just killed our brother and mother," Tyler responded.

"Y'all brother?" Tony said as he attempted to dive for the thirty-eight revolver he had on the dresser next to the bed. He never made it; the thunderous sound of the Colt Forty-Five Red had in his hand released fire into the fat man's ass as the bullet ripped his flesh open. Peaches lay there naked, scared that the next bullet would be hers.

"Wow, you were born with a hole in your ass, now you got two. Ain't that some shit," Tyler said in a joking manner while laughing at the fat man lying on the floor.

Big Tony was no longer being demanding since the boys had death written on them. He let out a faint whisper, "In the closet is a bag with well over two hundred thousand dollars and four kilos of cocaine. Just take it and leave, please, don't kill me."

Tyler moved to the closet and just like the fat man said, the bag was stuffed. After zipping the bag back up, Tyler turned back toward Red, who seemed to not even flinch as he held Big Tony and Peaches as gunpoint. "Looks like we're rich, Red," Tyler said as he threw the money bag in the middle of the floor. Red never said a word, just cracked a grin.

"You got the money, now just leave us alone," the fat man said angrily as the pain from his gunshot wound increased with every second.

"Oh we're gonna leave, but first, we're gonna play a game," Tyler said.

"What kind of game?" Tony said, stuttering the words out.

"First, Red, duct tape this fat fuck. I'm tired of hearing his mouth."

Red wasted no time taping the fat man up and giving him a kick in his ass for good measure. As Tony lay there helpless, they turn their attention to Peaches.

"Please, don't hurt me," Peaches said, almost in tears.

"Oh, we ain't gonna hurt you if you do what you're told," Tyler said as he smiled at Peaches. "So, you like to fuck, huh, Miss Peaches?" Tyler asked her.

Peaches thought to herself, *Maybe if I fuck them this will all be over.* "Do what you want to me, just don't kill me," Peaches said in her best scared voice.

Red, not saying a word, went to work duct taping both of Peaches' arms to the bed post. Peaches laid there with her legs open, actually turned on by what the young boys were about to do to her. Tyler climbed on the bed in between her thighs, sitting on his knees. To Peaches, it looked as if Tyler was reaching to undo his pants, and she actually was anticipating it. That was when she saw the .44 Bulldog coming out his waist line, giving her no time to move. Tyler shoved the cold steel deep in her wet pussy.

"You like to fuck, huh, bitch? Well, fuck this gun or I'm gonna kill you," Tyler demanded in the coldest voice she had ever heard. The thought that made her so wet now left her mind as the cold steel of the gun dug deep inside her pussy. The pain filled her with each stroke, but she never stopped praying it would be over with soon. Big Tony laid there as

Tyler fucked his wife with a pistol. All he could think of was how his man Slick would be returning to get him soon.

"I told you this bitch would fuck anything, Red."

Red laughed as he left the room, thinking about what was next for their victims. Peaches begged to herself that it would be over. She finally heard Tyler say, "That's enough," as he pulled the gun out of her now bleeding insides.

"Please, please don't kill me, I'm sorry," Peaches said, pleading for her life.

"Oh, we ain't gonna kill you," Tyler said with a devilish grin on his face.

Before Peaches knew it, Red walked back through the door carrying something she couldn't quite make out due to Tyler blocking her view. By the time she saw the hot iron Red held in his hand, it was inches from her face. Red pressed the iron down across the whole left side of her face. It was as if her flesh melted together, leaving her eye stuck closed permanently. The harder he pushed, the louder she screamed until the pain was so excruciating, she passed out. Big Tony's screams were muffled from the duct tape as the kingpin lay helpless praying, knowing that at any moment Slick should be walking through the door. Little did Tony know, Tyler and Red were hoping the same thing.

As the keys jingled in the door, Big Tony thought his prayers were finally answered. Surely, the young boys were no match for Slick. Slick struck fear in the heart of everyone in the city. Tyler and Red simultaneously jumped into the hiding positions and lay waiting for their next victim. Tony underestimated the wits of the young boys and he was helpless to warn Slick of the trap he was walking into.

"Boss!" Slick yelled from the living room as he made his way in the house. There was no response. Slick continued to walk toward the bedroom yelling, "Boss, you in there?" Still, no response. "Well, cover up so I can grab that bag." As he eased the door open, he wondered what that smell was in the air, not knowing that it was the smell of burnt flesh. He heard a muffled sound, causing him to look down and see his boss duct taped on the floor. "Boss, who the fuck did this?" Slick said nervously while noticing that the smell was Peaches. "Boss, are you okay?" he asked as he knelt down, pulling the tape from Big Tony's mouth. Before Big Tony could tell Slick to watch out, the whole top of his head seemed to pop off from the 44's blast, splashing Slick's brains and skull all over Big Tony. Laughter filled the air as Tyler and Red stood over their prey like animals. That was when Big Tony knew he was gonna die.

* * * * *

The next morning in the projects was one that would be remembered. As the projects woke, there was a scream outside that none would soon forget. The people ran to see what was going on. To everyone's surprise, stuck to the top of the pointy black fence rail was the head of Big Tony with what was later found out to be Slick's dick in his mouth.

As for Peaches, they didn't worry about her talking. Red took great pleasure in re-heating the iron and sealing her lips closed with it. They say the bitch killed herself a week later. As for Big Tony and Slick's bodies, they found them a month later in the trunk of a stolen car. Everyone in the projects knew who was responsible.

With two hundred and sixty-four thousand dollars and four kilos of cocaine, Taylor and Red wasted no time showing everybody who was in charge. Anybody that got in their way paid with their life. Within a week, the city was theirs. Even though Tyler was only fifteen, his street smarts were extraordinary. With Red killing relentlessly at his brother's side, the King was born.

As King stood over the casket of his only love, his anger engulfed him, knowing that vengeance must be his. Little did the world know, his plan was already underway. They stopped him the first time ten years ago, but this time they'd never have a chance.

As the casket of Queen was finally lowered in the ground, Twon and Qwon threw two roses on top of their mother's casket. When they looked up, there was their father.

"You got five minutes, Scott," the officer said, stepping back giving them time to talk.

"Twins, it's been a long time. I hope you're not mad at me for not letting y'all visit, but it was for your own good."

"We know, Pops," Qwon replied.

"Naw, we ain't mad. We're just happy to see you, even

though you all chained up," Twon added.

"Boys, I ain't got but a couple of minutes, so listen up. Did you get the key?"

"Yeah," they said simultaneously.

"Well, once you get the package I left you, look through it and find the folded piece of paper. It should have a key and an address. Go to it and wait there till you are contacted."

"Alright, Pops," they said.

"Don't look so sad, boys. We're gonna be together real soon. I love y'all."

"We love you, too," replied the boys.

"I got to go now, but trust me, everything is gonna make sense to y'all real soon. Be careful and always watch y'all back. Once you leave here, there is gonna be eyes on you, following you, trying to get what the fake ass police were looking for that night they took me away. So, once you get the package I left for you, protect its contents with your life."

Those were his last words as the guards escorted him off. In the distance, two white men in their mid-thirties were watching the whole conversation go down. They were wishing they could get closer and hoping to be able to report to the captain that they knew where King had hid the thing that would soon change the city.

The next morning, the two agents showed up at the group home Twon and Qwon were taken to. They were greeted at the front desk by Ms. Johnson.

"May I help you?" Ms. Johnson asked.

"Yes, you can. I'm Agent Reynolds and this is agent Phillips. We are with the DEA and we need to talk to Twon and Qwon Scott, please," the scrawny man said.

"Are they in trouble?" asked Ms. Johnson.

"No, ma'am, but it's important that we talk to them regarding their father," Philips said.

"Oh, right this way," Ms. Johnson said, leading them toward the twin's room. As she opened the door, to her surprise, the twins and their stuff were gone.

* * * * *

"Damn, Twon, hurry the fuck up. It's cold out here."

"Fuck you, I almost got it. This fucked up crowbar and your bitchin' ain't making matters no better," Twon replied as he gave the crowbar its last push, making the board that covered what used to be their kitchen pop loose. "I got it," Twon said, catching his breath.

"About fucking time, Twon. Move aside let a pro show you how it's done." Qwon kicked in the back door with ease.

"Your weak ass."

"Fuck you, Qwon." As the boys made their way in, it was almost as if the house hadn't changed since they moved out.

"Damn, we ain't been here in a while," Qwon said as they made their way into what was once their living room.

"Hell naw. It's hard to believe this is where it all started, huh?" Twon stated in a low voice.

It was ten years ago, the twins were only six. They were enjoying all the toys they received for Christmas when there was a beating at the door.

"Who is it?" King said.

"It's Benny," the voice said through the door.

Benny was King's capo and right hand man. King unlocked the door and as he turned the door knob, the door came flying in, pushing him back. Before he could say anything, he was looking down the barrel of a shot gun.

"Don't move, King, or I'll blow your fucking brains out," the young, plain clothed officer said as Benny and the two other white cops came in.

"Shut the door, Benny," the older, white guy said.

"What's this all about, Mike?" asked King, addressing the older, white officer in a confused voice.

"Benny here has been telling me that you got big plans and you haven't even consulted me about them. Shame on you, King. After all the stuff I do for you, this is how you repay me?"

"I don't know what you're talking about," King replied.

"Well, let me tell you what I'm talking about, you piece of shit. You have the recipe to a drug that is ten times more addictive than any drug. From what Benny has been telling me, you're gonna drop it on the white suburban areas and pull cocaine and heroin out of the hood. Who the fuck do you think you are—Robin Hood?"

"I still don't know what you are talking about," replied King.

"Okay, you wanna play? We are gonna search this house top to bottom, and if I don't find what we are here for, I'm gonna kill you and your family," said Mike.

"Benny, get the family out of here."

"Officer, hold them at gunpoint. If they move, kill 'em," said Mike.

Queen and the kids didn't know what was going on as Benny rounded them up and sat them down on the living room couch next to King. As Benny stood there, he tried his best not to look King in his eyes.

"Benny, I can't believe you," King finally said before Benny walked away to help with the search.

"I can't believe you, King. You can't stop selling drugs in the hood. What the fuck am I gonna do then, huh? That's why I told Mike about your plan. He can have that bullshit drug you think can change the world and with you out of the way, I'll be the new king," Benny replied. King sat there and never said a word as Benny walked off. As they sat on the couch, the young officer held the shot gun on them.

"How long have you known Agent Mike Fellows?" King asked in a military like voice. The young agent wouldn't respond, but King pressed on. "He's a dirty fucka, ain't he?" King asked, thinking about how he met Agent Fellows.

Agent Fellows was worse than crooked, and he had

connects to judges, which he found to be an advantage after King took over the city. It wasn't long before Agent Fellows came to King with a proposition. He remembered Agent Fellows saying, "You can sell what you want so long as I get a cut and you keep it in the hood. In return, I'll keep all heat off you. You got a problem? I'll fix it, but if you cross me, I'll destroy you, you understand?" King wasted no time accepting the FBI on the payroll. *Who can fuck with you?* the King thought as he stared down the barrel of this shot gun as the same man he made a deal with searched his fuckin' house. *Stupid fucks, they will never find it.*

King never took his eyes off the young officer, watching for any chance to make a move. It finally came when the officer was distracted by a crashing sound from upstairs. He looked back, but never got a chance to turn around as the Desert Eagle came from under the couch cushion. King wasted no time squeezing the trigger, sending the bullet spiraling toward the young officer, finally slamming into the officer's face as he dropped to the floor. It was as if the whole bottom part of his face disappeared. His body shook frantically as the young man took his last breath. Queen grabbed the twins and took them to the kitchen out of harm's way. She dialed 911 as quickly as she could

"911, what's your emergency?" the operator said.

In a frantic voice, Queen replied, "An officer has been shot, send help right away!" She then hung up the phone. By then, they had traced the call and should be on their way.

King retreated also to the kitchen as Agent Fellows and Benny made their way down the stairs. They noticed the officer that once held the shotgun was part of the floor.

"King, come out!" Agent Fellows yelled.

"Fuck you. You thought you could come in here and take King out like that. If anybody come in this kitchen, they gonna end up like your friend on the floor," King stated before he started laughing.

As Agent Fellows thought about his next move, the sirens in the distance helped him out. "Benny, get the fuck out of here and let me handle this," Agent Fellows said in a nervous voice. Benny wasted no time getting gone.

When the police pulled up, Agent Fellows met them on the porch. "King is in the kitchen, he is armed and we got one officer down in the living room," stated Agent Fellows.

"Tyler Scott, put the weapon down and come out of the kitchen," the unit officer said as his men took their positions in the living room. As they noticed the young agent on the floor dead, one officer had to do his best not to throw up.

"I'm gonna give up, my lawyer's on the way. I'm throwing my gun out," King said as he slid the firearm across the floor. He then walked out with his hands up, and the officers took him into custody.

Queen and the twins watched as they took the King away from them in cuffs. The twins were only six years old and stood there angry as little tears ran down their faces. Who would think ten years later they would be standing in the same spot.

"Come on, Qwon, let's get what we are here for and get the fuck out of here," Twon said.

"I'm witcha, Bro," Qwon replied.

Their bedroom looked the same, just dusty. They wasted no time turning their focus on Michael Jordan painted on the wall. They remembered they couldn't go in their room for a week until it was done. Now, they stood face to face to it, wondering what was behind it. As they put their hand on the wall, they noticed it felt different than the rest of the wall. It was made from dry wall.

"Let me see the crowbar, Twon," Qwon said. Within seconds, he slammed it into the wall and to their surprise, a hole emerged.

* * * * *

"Tyler Scott, Tyler Scott, you got a visit," the fat officer yelled. As they made their way down the hallway, King already knew who his visitor was and couldn't hide the grin on his face. As the private visiting room door buzzed open, there sat Agent Fellows.

"I don't remember seeing you on my visiting list," King said as he took a seat at the table.

"I see you haven't lost your sense of humor in ten years in this shit hole," Agent Fellows replied, cracking a smile.

"What the fuck do you want?" King said as he sat back in his chair.

"I'll tell you what the fuck I want. I want you to know that I will personally be at your appeal hearing this week to make sure you never leave this place. It just so happens that the judge is a very close friend of mine, and you know how friends stick together, don't you, King? You don't since the only friend you had took your place and now works for me. All you had to do was play by my rules and you could've had everything, but you are too smart for your own good." King never said anything; he just sat there as if the agent wasn't even talking to him. The whole time, he knew his plan was underway, and Agent Mike Fellows or any crooked ass judge couldn't stop it.

King sat forward in his seat and said in a nice voice, "I enjoyed your visit, Agent Fellows, but it's time for me to go. But, don't worry, we will have a chance to visit again real soon." King pushed his chair away from the table, and then stood up and made his way to the door.

"Guard!" King yelled as the fat, white man reappeared, opening the door and letting him out. Agent Fellows sat there for a few minutes alone, thinking back to when King made him so much money he didn't know what to do with it all. *Benny keeps my pockets fat, but he sure ain't no King. King is too fucking smart and powerful, which is why I can't never let him get out of here alive.*

* * * * *

As the hole emerged bigger with each strike of the

crowbar, light begin to shine on what was behind the wall, revealing what they could start to make out to be some kind of safe. Qwon dropped the crowbar and they began pulling the drywall away with their hands until they stood looking at the safe that had been hidden in the walls for over ten years.

"Qwon, where is the key?" Twon could barely get the words out of his mouth before Qwon had stuck the key in the lock and turned it. Twon turned the handle almost simultaneously, pulling the safe door open. In the safe was a big black bag.

Qwon grabbed it and pulled it out. "Damn, this bag is heavy as hell," Qwon said in a somewhat strained voice as he dropped it to the floor in front of him. Twon bent down and opened the zipper. As he pulled it back, they couldn't help but see the money that seemed to jump out of the bag at them.

"Shit, Twon, look at all the money," Qwon said as his eyes got as big as silver dollars.

Twon reached down to make sure it was real. They wasted no time pulling out stack by stack, the money which was neatly wrapped with money bonds which told them how much each stack was. When the money was on the floor, they had counted five hundred thousand dollars.

"Qwon, we rich." Twon said, trying to calm down.

"Hell yeah. I'm gonna buy Jordan's for the rest of my life. Shit, what else is in the bag?"

Twon reached in, and pulled out two long black cases and

an envelope.

"That's it," Twon said as he handed the cases to his brother. Qwon noticed that each case was labeled with their names.

"Huh, this one is yours, Twon," Qwon said as they opened the cases together.

They couldn't believe what they saw. The looked at each other, then looked backed down at what seemed to be a treasure. Each case contained two twin gold plated Desert Eagles, and engraved in them were their names, Prince Twon and Prince Qwon. Living in the projects, they had seen their share of guns, but none like those.

"Twon, see what's in the envelope," Qwon said as he stood up, holding both guns and aiming at the wall. Twon ripped the envelope open as he grabbed the papers out of it. The key their father told them about fell out onto the floor. Twon opened the papers. The first one had a bunch of words and numbers on it. It looked like some kind of code or something. Twon went to the next paper.

"Twon, what was that?" Qwon said, putting the guns back in their cases.

"I don't know, it looks like some kind of code or something."

As Twon flipped to the next page, it had an address at the top: 1622 Harmony Lane, and under it read:

If you boys are reading this, then I'm either dead or in jail. Whatever the situation, you have no time to waste. The paper you have with the crazy writing on it you must protect it with your lives. I know you don't understand what's going on right now, but you soon will. Hurry and go to the address. Make sure you're not followed. The money is for y'all, but that's nothing compared to what your future will bring y'all...King.

Qwon started packing the money up as Twon flipped to the last paper in his hand

"It's a birth certificate," Twon said, looking confused.

"A what?"

"You heard me, a birth certificate, but it ain't neither one of ours. It says Latisha Scott, born January 10th, 1975 to Debra and Tyler Scott."

"What the fuck is going on? Momma ain't never saying nothing about no sister," Qwon said.

"Hell naw, she must have died at birth," Qwon said, trying to make up a logical excuse. "Fuck it, Twon, let's get the fuck out of here," Qwon said, picking up the bag and turning toward the door, and that's when they heard it—the back door open and close.

"Twon, Qwon, we know you're in here," a voice yelled from downstairs. "We don't want to hurt you, we just wanna talk. We're federal agents," Agent Phillips said as he waived Agent Reynolds to go in the living room as he covered him.

"Qwon, what are we gonna do now?" Twon said in a whisper.

"I got a plan," he replied as he sat the bag back down and started to unzip it.

"Reynolds, you hear that? I think they're upstairs, let's go!" Phillips said, pointing to the stairs. Before they could take a step, the thunderous sound of Qwon's Desert Eagle filled the house. The agents dove back in the kitchen as bullets whizzed past them, slamming into the wall and barely missing their target.

"Where you going, mu'fuckas!" Qwon yelled as he let off two more rounds.

"Put the gun down before somebody gets hurt!" Agent Phillips yelled back, now covered where the bullets couldn't reach him.

"What y'all here for?" asked Qwon.

"We just wanna talk, but you're gonna have to put the gun down," the agent said.

"Fuck y'all, I can hear you from there. Now, talk," said Qwon. Phillips was left no choice but to start talking.

"We're not here to hurt y'all. We believe you got something we're looking for and if you just give it to us, we'll leave and y'all can go about y'all business." The agent got no response.

"Enough playing games, Phillips, let's take these little bastards. Nobody will miss them," said Reynolds. Phillips grinned to his partner, enjoying the thought of killing the twins.

"Cover me," Phillips said as he started making his way back into the living room with extreme caution.

They were making their way to the stairs again. They

were through talking and death was all they could think about as they made their way to the top of the stairs. The bathroom door was open directly in front of them to their right. A bedroom door was open as well, but to their left was the twin's room with the door shut. They secured the rooms behind them before approaching the closed door. The agents took no more chances. They aimed at the door and opened fire with the department issued .40 cals. In a matter of seconds, the door was ate up with gaping holes the size of baseballs. The door barely crept open as the agents reloaded, hoping the silence meant they had hit their targets. Agent Reynolds, with his gun out in front of him, stood with his back against the wall by the entrance to the room, hoping his next step wouldn't be his last. Phillips was crouched down, moving slowly into the room as he made his way. His eyes got as big as the holes in the door, and Reynolds looked down, seeing the expression on his partner's face. That's when he heard the sound that would change everything for them.

January 7, 2002

With only two days until court, King laid in his cell thinking about the last ten years of his life. In ten years, he got one visit and that was from his beloved Queen. That was when he first got there. After that visit, Queen never came back at his request. She knew why, because there was too much at stake and she didn't want to jeopardize the plan. Life in jail wasn't hard for the King. He had privileges that only money could buy—women, drugs, liquor, you name it, and he got it. His cell wasn't with the rest of the inmates; it was by itself on the wing at the prison no longer used. His cell was two cells combined. He had carpeted floors, big screen TV, and, of course, his king sized bed. The only thing King couldn't buy was his freedom. He had to turn his back on his family in order to protect them. The night he killed that officer, he knew what they were looking for and he also knew that once they didn't find it, they would surely kill him and his family with no hesitation. For the secret King had, you could end up dead or in jail. So, instead of waiting on them to decide, he decided jail. With him in jail, his secret was safe. Nobody knew where it was but him and Queen. Even though her addition got the best of her, she would rather die than betray her family. The thoughts of the Queen always touched a spot in his heart that nobody but her knew existed in him. Those brown eyes, those pretty brown eyes. *Soon, love, they will all pay*, the King thought as he closed his eyes and went to sleep, knowing the plan was underway.

As Agent Reynolds stood above his partner gripping his .40 cal as tightly as he could, the next noise was undeniable. It was one that let him know that they had made a terrible error in judgment. Agent Phillips seemed to have frozen in his tracks, knowing it was too late. *Skiiiiiiirt.* It was a sound they had heard so many times before. It was the sound of their Crown Vic peeling out of the driveway. Cops usually always left their car running, especially when it was as cold as it was outside. That time it cost them big.

"Those fuckin' niggers done climbed out of the window and stole our fuckin' car!" Phillips shouted to his partner as he ran to the open window that was previously boarded up. As he looked out the window, he saw exactly how they got from the second floor to the ground. The garage was right under their window, and that was an easy jump for two young boys of their age running for their lives.

"Fuck, Phillips, the safe is empty. What the fuck are we gonna tell Fellows? He's gonna have our ass for this."

"I don't know, but we gotta get to a phone fast," Phillips said, realizing their phones were in the car. They holstered their weapons and headed for the stairs looking disgusted, knowing they would surely kill the twins with great pleasure once they caught them. As they made their way down the stairs and across the living room, Phillips couldn't help but think to himself, *Didn't we leave the door open?* but he brushed it off as his cop instinct was working overtime. Too bad it was working on the wrong thing, because they never heard the hallway closet open as they passed it.

"Y'all just wanted to talk, huh? Well, I hate to be rude and not talk back," Twon said as he stood behind the agents with both guns aimed at their targets.

The agents would have never guessed that one of the boys had doubled back and waited on them as they searched upstairs trying to kill the twins. The agents never got the chance to turn around before Twon let off eight shots of thunder, four from each gun, and all the bullets hit their targets. Reynolds caught the worst of the gunfire. One shot completely smashed in the back of his head, and three more buried in his back. He was dead before he hit the ground. Phillips took two slugs high in his back, with the force from the impact completely spinning him around until he found himself sitting on his ass in the middle of the kitchen.

"You fucking nigger, you shot me!" Phillips said in a grimacing voice as he felt his body. Twon walked closer to the fallen agent, avoiding his partner's brains that were leaking all over the floor, until he was standing over Phillips looking down at him.

"You're going to jail for life, you little shit, just like your fath…" Phillips never got the chance to finish his sentence before the whole right side of his face seemed to disappear from the eight rounds Twon squeezed off into Phillip's face.

"Fuck you, pussy," was all Twon said as he put up his smoking guns and made his way out of the back door to his brother waiting in the agents' car.

"Hurry up and close the door, it's cold outside mu'fucka," Qwon said as he pulled away from the curb.

"Fuck you, you could be as cold as them two fuckas in the house," Town replied. They both started laughing as they headed for their next destination.

"The gas attendant said to keep straight for five to ten miles out of the city limits and to play close attention because the street signs are hard to spot. He also said he didn't understand why anybody would want to go out there—it's nothing but a bunch of abandoned warehouses," Qwon said as he sped off down the road in search of Harmony Lane.

After damn near twenty minutes, Twon finally spotted it.

"That's it, Qwon, right there," Twon said as he pointed toward a narrow road that looked like it led to nowhere.

After five minutes on the dirt road, they could see in the distance the warehouse the gas station attendant was talking about. As they approached, they looked nervously at the three buildings that stood in the middle of nowhere. The Crown Vic came to an abrupt stop in front of the biggest of the three buildings.

"1-6-22, right?" Qwon asked as he squinted to see the numbers on the building.

"Yeah, that's it, but you don't have to stop the car like you crazy. If you would have made me hit my head, I would have fucked you up," Twon said.

"Whatever, get your ass out of the car and let's check this place out," Qwon replied as he got out of the car.

"This shit look crazy," Qwon said as he looked around.

"Man, bring your sorry ass on," Twon replied as he turned and headed toward the building.

As they reached the door, they were unable to look through the windows. They seemed to be covered with paint. As they opened the door and stepped inside, the only lighting that came in through the skylight offered little help as the sun was just about to go down. They could barely make out the maze of pallets damn near stacked to the ceiling.

"We gotta find some light, I can barely see shit," Twon said.

"I hope this old ass place got some light. If not, what we gonna do then?"

"I don't know, we'll worry about that later. We wasting

time now because the sun is going completely down in a few minutes. Let's split up and get to looking," Twon answered.

"Yeah, you're right, but be careful. I gotta funny feeling about this place," said Qwon.

"Now who's scared, wit' your soft ass."

"Fuck you, Twon, just be careful, a'ight?"

"Yeah, yeah, whatever," Twon replied as he made his way toward the left side of the warehouse, leaving Qwon no choice but to take the right.

Twon made his way through the maze, working cautiously. He couldn't help but worry if his brother was okay. He was trying to stay focused on the task at hand when he heard a noise that made him stop and listen.

"Qwon, is that you?" Twon said, but there was no response.

Twon wasted no time pulling one of his guns from his waistline as he continued to the end of the row. There, to his left, was a stairway and on that wall next to the bottom of the stairs looked to be a power box. All he could think was, *Please, let this shit work.* As he approached the box, the lever was down in the off position, so Twon grabbed the rusty handle and pushed it up, and within seconds the once dark warehouse was full of light. Twon's relief only lasted for a second as he felt the cold feeling of steel pressed against the back of his head and heard a voice that was even colder.

"Drop the fucking gun before I put your brains all over that wall," the grimy voice demanded.

Twon wasted not a second letting it hit the ground, knowing whoever it was had caught his ass slipping for real.

"Nigga, if you don't get that gun off my brother's head, you gonna die where you stand," Qwon said as he stood holding both his cannons pointed at the stranger that held his brother at gunpoint.

"A'ght, shorty, be easy, don't get jumpy. I didn't mean any harm," the man replied as he raised his hands up in a surrendering motion. Twon was sure happy to hear his brother. He thought for sure he was about to die.

"Now, give me a reason why I shouldn't kill you, mu' fucka?" Qwon asked the man as his fingers itched to pull the triggers.

The man started laughing as he gave his answer. "I'll tell you why, twins, 'cause I'm your Uncle Red."

* * * * *

A whisper was all he heard as King sat on the edge of his bed. "They're gonna try and kill you when you go to court," the whispering voice said. All King could hear were the footsteps walking away as he lay back on his bed, knowing death was around the corner.

* * * * *

The twins hadn't seen their Uncle Red since they were eight years old, but they weren't deaf to the stories they'd heard about him in the streets. Red was one of the most dangerous men alive in the city. Heartless, cold blooded, and, not to mention, he had the natural instincts of a hit man. Nobody crossed King or Red without getting a visit from death. Once Red was on your trail, there was no getting away. After King and Red took the throne from Big Tony, Red killed anybody that stood in their way. If you weren't with them, you were dead. If you were late with money, you were dead. If you talked to the police, you most definitely were dead. Once King got locked up, Red disappeared into the shadows of the city, and ten years later he stood in a warehouse laughing at his nephews.

"Uncle Red!" the boys said simultaneously as most twins did. He wasn't as big as their father, but they looked almost identical from the long braids that covered their heads to the gold trims that covered their teeth. You knew they were brothers. Red's skin tone was a few shades lighter than King's, but he stood six-four like his brother.

"Damn, I ain't seen y'all since y'all was this high," Red said, holding his hand down by his thigh. "Now look at y'all all grown up and shit. Well, I know y'all got a lot of questions, but we ain't got a lot of time, so the questions are gonna have to wait until later. Let's roll, we got shit to do."

The boys never said a word, they just followed their uncle through the lit warehouse, wondering to themselves what the fuck was going on.

* * * * *

Agent Fellows sat impatiently in his office as his secretary walked in. "Sir, Phillips and Reynolds aren't answering their phones, and nobody has heard from them since this morning," his secretary stated.

"Well, keep calling," Fellows snapped back at his secretary as he pointed toward the door for her to leave. As soon as the door closed, Fellows pulled out his cell phone and begin dialing. The phone rang until a deep, hoarse sounding voice answered on the other end.

"Yeah," the voice answered.

"They'll be moving him at three a.m. as a precaution for his safety. You'll only have one chance, so don't fuck this up," Agent Fellows said as he hit the end button on his phone. There weren't too many people that got away with talking to the Reaper like that, but Mike Fellows was one of them.

The Reaper had been killing for the last fifteen years. He was known as the best hit man out there. He was a real favorite of the Mafia and had made so much money from them that he was set for life. But, it wasn't about money with him anymore, it was the thrill of the kill. It was what he called an art in the way he brought death upon someone. Once, he was on the sixtieth floor of a building washing windows like an average window washer. When he saw his victim sit down at his desk in front of his computer, that was when his signature AR-15 made quick work of the window and the victim. By the time people realized what happened, he'd vanished. Now, he sat in his hotel room studying a picture of his next victim, King.

Transporting King always seemed like a big event, even at three a.m. in the morning. He was chained and cuffed, and then put in the back of the unmarked van. Two black Suburbans escorted the van, one in the front and one in the back. Each was filled with four SWAT team members armed and ready for war.

"We almost ready," the gray haired captain said to the caravan.

The deputy driving the van responded in an inpatient voice, "We're just waiting on the two marshals that are supposed to ride in back with the prisoner, but they're late, as usual."

At that very moment, in walked the marshals – a heavy set white man, along with his pretty brown partner. "I'm sorry we're late. I'm Jones, this is Sullivan," the lady marshal said as they made their way toward the van.

"Well, I'm happy you could join us, Jones and Sullivan. Let's get the show on the road," the captain said as he closed the Suburban door and gave the signal to open the garage.

They were about forty minutes from the city on a clear day, but it was beginning to snow so they'd have to drive a little slower, which meant it may take them an extra thirty minutes. The ride was actually smoother than they expected as they got off on the exit ramp that led into the city. As they were coming down the hill toward the underpass, they could see flares by the roadside and a police car up ahead. They thought someone was not as lucky as them. As they approached, they saw an officer standing in the icy road putting out road flares. You could clearly see a collision ahead at the four-way stop light. It was a van and a Camaro. The driver of the van looked to be alright while he talked to the flare officer's partner. The driver of the Camaro had clearly gone through the windshield of his car and was lying in the street, covering the freshly fallen snow with blood. The caravan slowly came to a halt as the flare officer approached the first black Suburban.

"What happened?" the captain said, letting down his window to talk to the officer.

"Looks like a DUI. There is a bottle of liquor on the front seat of the van," the officer replied.

"Is there anything we can do?" asked the captain.

"Naw, we got EMS in route as we speak, so if you could just bear with us for a few minutes, we'll have you on your way," the officer said.

"No problem, just know we're in a bit of a hurry," the white haired captain said as he let the window back up to keep the heat in. He then got on his radio to let the caravan know what was going on. "We're gonna be here for a few, so make yourself comfortable, but stay alert," the captain said.

Everything looked safe as they sat there. There was nobody out at three forty a.m. but the few homeless people that lived under the ramp that were huddled around a fire that

JOE AWSUM

burned out of a barrel. The captain sipped his coffee, thinking about how he was gonna go home and get some sleep when it was all over. The flare officer called for his partner to come over to the police car that sat to the side of the road. Once he reached the car, his partner was digging in the trunk like he was looking for another road flare. A suspected drunk man stood in the road, waiting for the officer to come back and finish taking his statement. The flare officer looked to have found what he was looking for, but to the captain's surprise, it wasn't flair, it was an AR-15. The flare officer wasted no time unleashing on the second Suburban. They never saw it coming, and they never had a chance as the shooters accuracy seemed to rip through everyone in the Suburban in a matter of seconds. The captain's frantic cries of ambush were useless. His eyes showed a clear sign of panic as he looked forward and saw that the bloody body that lay in the street was aiming an AK-47 at his Suburban. The so called DUI suspect was holding what looked to be a Teck Nine. Before the captain could react, gunfire filled him and the driver. The right back passenger was hit in the neck that left blood squirting everywhere. The remaining SWAT member tried to open his door and step out, butthe AK fire almost took his leg completely off, making him fall flat on his face. The driver and passenger of the van tried their best to return fire, but the AR-15 was turned on them, slicing through their limbs, making quick work of them.

"Don't kill me!" the almost legless SWAT officer cried as

the flare officer's partner stood over him aiming his Glock Nine at him. Two loud pops were all you heard as the SWAT officer took his last breath. A dead silence took the air except for three homeless men that were once in front of the fire. One of them pushed his basket full of cans across the street, moving fast toward where the assassin with the AK stood.

"Get the fuck out of here," the AK wielding man yelled to the bum.

All he saw was the shining gold from the man's grill and a flash from the .357 that Red had pulled from under his rags that sent a bullet smack in the middle of the assassin's forehead. The man with the Tech couldn't react fast enough to get out of the way of the three slugs that hit him center mass. Red moved for cover swiftly as the AR-15 spit in his direction, barely missing him. The flare officer and his partner shot relentlessly at their target, but their key mistake was not paying attention to the two bums that crept up behind them holding twin Desert Eagles. The bark from the golden eagles ripped off rounds in the assassins until they were empty and the top part of the guns set cocked back, waiting for them to feed them another clip. As the gunfire stopped, the marshals in the back of the van sat as if nothing had happened outside. Sullivan, the heavyset white man, sat there and lit a Marlboro, and then he began to speak as he blew the smoke out.

"Well, King, long time no see. Too bad it has to be on these terms," Sullivan said.

"I agree, Sullivan, or would you like to be called the Reaper now?" replied King.

"I see you haven't lost your touch for surprises," replied Sullivan.

"I guess this is the part where you kill me, huh?" replied King, showing no fear in his eyes.

"Actually, it's not," replied Sullivan. "I would like to introduce you to my promising new protégée', Ms. Aisha. I thought I'd give her the honors of this one."

Ms. Aisha had been the number one hitter in the Reaper's Death Squad. She seemed to come out nowhere seven months ago and displayed a killer's instinct that made the Reaper cuff her and take her under his wing while teaching her everything he knew.

"Well, King, I can't say it was nice knowing you. I never did like you. I'm gonna enjoy watching you die. Aisha, if you would do the honors," Sullivan said.

Ms. Aisha wasted no time pulling her .45 out and aiming it at her target.

"Twins, y'all alright?" Uncle Red asked as he ran toward them. They never got a chance to answer before they heard a single gunshot go off inside the van. They ran to the van, Red grabbed the door handle. The twins stood there pointing their guns toward the doors. Red pulled the door open and what they saw made their heart skip a beat. They never moved as the large man fell to the ground with a bullet in his head. Aisha stood there, gun smoking, looking like she had no mercy in her anywhere. The boys took aim, and Uncle Red never moved out the way. He just looked down at the body in front of him. Amazed, the large man was still holding his cigarette.

"Now, y'all kids play nice," King said as he stood up in the line of fire between the twins and Ms. Aisha. "Twins, I'd like y'all to meet your sister, Latisha Scott." The twins lowered their guns with a look of confusion on their face as they watched their sister put her gun down and hug their father.

"Enough for the family reunion. Twon, go get the car, Qwon, get the gasoline, and, Tish, get your father out of them cuffs and shackles. Let's get the fuck out of here," Red said. He could hear sirens in the distance.

As they pulled away up the ramp, all that was left was a blazing inferno that would take hours to put out. Plus, it would take another two months to go through all the dental records to realize the King was gone. The King couldn't help but think to himself, *I've waited ten years for this moment, and now that I'm free it is time to punish the people that oppressed my black people for hundreds of years. The people that fed us crack cocaine and heroin, and watched us sit back and destroy ourselves and our families with addictions we can't control - the police, the judges, and the prosecutors that throw our young, black men in jail and never give them a second chance at redemption. But, now the time has come that they will all bow down to the royal family, and all our loyal followers.* All he could do was grin as they sped off to their destiny.

Part Two

Family Over Everything

By nine a.m., the scene of the fire was a complete chaos with fire trucks, police, Feds, U.S. Marshals, and, of course, the media. The fire fighters fought for two hours to put the blaze out and when it was, there were a lot of unanswered questions. What seemed to be the main question was if King was dead or alive, but nobody had the answers and with all the charred remains, they were not gonna know anytime soon. The news had a field day with the story from one station to the next.

"Was this an assassination or an escape?" one reporter reported.

A black man reported, "Long live the King."

Everybody had their own opinion. It hadn't been that much speculation since the late Tupac Shakur. Nobody knew at that very moment that on the outskirts of town in a warehouse, the beginning stages of producing The Beast was already underway. Actually, they'd been underway for over a month.

"Professor, how is everything coming along?" the King asked as he looked at the elderly man hitting vodka from his flask.

"I'm coming along fine, can't you tell?" the man responded jokingly as he took another sip.

The professor was once a prominent doctor of medicine. He even graduated from Harvard Medical School head of his class. He worked for a major hospital for years until they found out he was selling prescriptions to people in the hood who couldn't afford them. After he was fired, he turned his life into helping people that couldn't go the hospital—mostly criminals with gunshot wounds and that was how he met King.

One night, King had to acquire his services when Red got shot in the back by a rival gang, and he took care of Red— no questions asked, which was how King liked it. Being in the business King was in, he sent the professor all kinds of business. The only thing was the man always had farfetched stories. Most people just thought he was crazy and drunk, but not King. King took a great interest in the Professor and his stories, especially the one about him being able to create a drug so powerful it would change the world. The Professor sometimes drank, but, in fact, was a genius.

He created a small blue pellet that you placed on your tongue that instantly dissolved. Within seconds, you would be on a high that you could only imagine for the next two hours. Your high would increase to the point you thought you couldn't take it anymore, and that was when the hallucinations would kick in. They would soon turn to nightmares. What scared the person the most was that even once the high wore off, the nightmares would continue and the only way to escape them was to start all over again. Soon, you'd need more as your body got used to it. The beauty of it was to make one thousand pellets would only cost fifty dollars and the ingredients were easy to acquire in mass amounts without drawing attention. The only problem was the Professor needed money, equipment, and a big place to start production. That was where King came in. The pellet sounded good to King, but he had to see it in action first.

The Professor quickly obliged him by telling King to bring him a test dummy of his choice. The next day, the King returned with a stoner named Rick that was into every drug under the sun. For him to try some new shit, he couldn't wait. The Professor gave Rick the little pellet the size of a BB, and Rick took it, looking at it like he was saying, *"I came all this way for this little shit?"* But, he did as instructed and placed it on his tongue. He couldn't even taste anything as it quickly dissolved as promised, and the next thing Rick knew he was so high he thought his heart would come out of his chest, run around the room and jump back in.

After about forty minutes, he could of swore he seen it happen, but really the hallucinations had kicked in, meaning his high was coming down. Once his high wore off, Rick couldn't do anything but ask where he could get some more of that shit. Yeah, it passed the first test, but King was more interested in the second test—the nightmares. Like the Professor said, it happened.

Rick called King sounding like he'd been running from a monster or something. He was claiming that his Dad was back from the grave and had been trying to kill him. But, that wasn't why he was calling, because the last thing he said was, "Do you think I could get another one of those pellets?"

At that moment, King knew he had to act fast, so he told the Professor he had a deal, but he needed the ingredients and how to make it written down and coded. That way, only the two of them could read it. The Professor looked nervous about that idea at first, until King opened a suitcase with one hundred thousand dollars in it. The Professor jumped on the money.

King told the man, "Pack your stuff, you're moving." That was before King was arrested. So, for the last thirteen and a half years, King hid the Professor away. Now, the white haired, little black man with his wire glasses stood before him mass producing what King called "The Beast".

"Things are right on schedule with this expensive equipment you've purchased and a whole warehouse full to the ceiling with supplies. I could supply the whole United States in less than six months," the Professor said.

"That's what I like to hear, 'cause by the end of the week we start distribution," replied King. But, in the meantime, King thought it was best to go talk with the twins and his daughter about what was going on, and get them ready for the road that lied ahead of them.

* * * * *

"Man, you ain't shot shit," said Twon.

"You crazy as hell, I'm a mu'fuckin' killa, nigga," Qwon said as he made his motion like he was shooting his brother.

"You ain't no killa shooting with your eyes closed," said Twon.

"You wasn't saying that shit the other day when Uncle Red caught your ass slippin'," said Qwon.

"Fuck you," said Twon.

"Fuck wit' me," said Qwon.

"You both need to chill out," Latisha said, jumping in the conversation between her brothers.

"Fuck you, too," the boys said simultaneously to their sister.

"I got y'all fuck you right here," she said as she stood up and pulled her .45 out of her Gucci purse, and took aim at her brothers. The boys wasted no time grabbing their guns off the table and taking aim back at their sister. As King walked in the big warehouse where the twins met their uncle for the first time, he could see Red walking toward him laughing.

"Red, what you laughing?" said King.

"Your kids, nigga, and if I was you, I'd hurry up and get to the office before they kill each other…Dad," Red said to his brother and burst out laughing even harder than before.

"Fuck you, Red." King replied as he hurried to the office.

"If y'all fools don't put them guns down," King said in a voice that only a father possessed. The guns hit the table as quickly as they took them up.

"Dad, they started it," said Aisha.

"Pops, she lying, she pulled her gun out first," Qwon said, pointing to his sister.

King couldn't help but laugh to himself as he looked at his children. The twins reminded himself of him when he was younger. Six feet, 360 degrees of waves, naturally fit, and the eyes of stone cold killers, and then there was Latisha, his baby girl and a spittin' image of her mother, but he knew behind that puppy dog look on her face was a black widow.

You see, when Queen found out she was pregnant with a girl, King sent her away to stay with her sister until she had the baby. At that time in life, King and Red were at war with everybody and King couldn't risk anyone knowing he had a child. He knew that would be his weakness and when you were on top, you couldn't afford any weaknesses. Once Latisha was born, she stayed with her auntie. Even though the Queen was hurt about leaving her baby, she knew she had to change. It was for her own safety.

Latisha grew up as a normal child. She was well taken

care of by her Auntie Rose, who she thought was her mother. King and Queen made sure she never wanted for anything. The only bad part was that Aunt Rose spent a lot of the money she was given and kept a revolving door of niggas.

By the age of fourteen, Latisha already looked like a little woman. She had been wearing a bra since she was twelve, and those same hips her mother had were poking out. One night, Aunt Rose was having her regular get together and her boyfriend for the week, Larry, chose that night to make the move he'd been thinking about all day as he watched Latisha walk around in her tight shorts. Once everybody was drunk, he excused himself from the party like he was going to the bathroom, instead, he made a detour to Latisha's room. Before she knew what was happening, the man was on top of her with his pants down. His right hand covered her mouth and his left hand held the knife to her face, and dared her to move. He tried to penetrate her as the tears ran down her face, wishing it was over. Latisha was still a virgin and her tightness prevented her attacker from pushing inside her. Within a second, the man ejaculated all over her panties. He told her if she told anybody about what happened, he'd kill her and her mother, who she thought was Rose at that time. He then pulled his pants up, left out of the room, and went back to the party like nothing happened. Latisha laid there crying and scared to move.

When the morning came, Latisha showered for about an hour in the hottest water she could stand. She scrubbed and scrubbed, but she still felt dirty. She quickly got dressed, grabbed her school bag, and was out the door. She tried not to bump into her auntie going to work, and she sure didn't want to see Larry. Latisha walked to the school, but never went inside. Instead, she walked to the park and sat on the swing, but never swung. She just sat there and cried in her hands until she was startled by approaching footsteps and a voice she'd never forget.

"Are you alright?" the voice said.

"I'm fine," Latisha said, looking up at the man. She couldn't help but wonder where he'd come from.

"I mean, you are over here crying all alone. Is there something you want to talk about?"

"Who are you—some kind of guardian or something? What, you just walk around all day looking for females that are crying? If it will make you leave me alone, I'll tell you what's wrong with me. I got raped, okay….are you happy now?" She couldn't even look up at the man.

"Latisha, who raped you?" the man demanded.

"How do you know my name? I never told you my name," she replied in a sobbing voice as she looked and saw fury in the man's eyes.

"Who?" was all the man said. That time she asked no more questions.

"My mom's boyfriend, Larry."

"Where is he at right now?" the man asked.

"Probably at the house still sleep, but, but, I'm not

supposed to tell anybody or else he's gonna kill me," Latisha said with a scared look on her face.

"Let's go, it's time we have a few words with Larry," replied the man.

Even though he was a stranger to her, she stood up and followed the man to his car. There was just something about him that made her feel safe, but it sure wasn't the gold trims that he had on his teeth.

Just like she said, Larry was still in the bed and sound asleep, but it didn't last long as the stranger grabbed Larry out of the bed by his neck and dragged him in the living room, kicking and trying to scream. Once the stranger let him go, he sat in the middle of the floor, looking like he wanted to kill somebody.

"This is my house mu'fucka, you best get the fuck ou…"

He never got to finish his sentence before he found himself looking down the barrel of a .357.

"Now that I have your attention, you piece of shit, the best advice I could give you right now is to shut the fuck up and listen. Out of all the females in the world, you chose this one to put your filthy hands on," the stranger said.

"I…I…I… wouldn't do that," Larry said in a pleading voice, looking at Latisha, who was standing behind her guardian angel with tears of anger coming down her face.

"If you say one more fucking word, I'll kill you dead, bitch. I can't believe you put your hands on my niece, nigga.

I should kill you myself, but I got a better plan. Come here, Latisha. It's alright, your Uncle Red ain't gonna let nothing happen to you, baby; I promise."

Since King was in jail, Red's job was to watch over Latisha day and night without her knowing, and there he was passing the gun to his niece. Latisha was nervous, but she held the big gun.

"That's it, hold it with both hands," Red said, guiding his niece.

"Latisha, I was drunk. I'll never touch you again, I promise. I made a mistake," pleaded Larry.

"You fucking right you made a mistake," Latisha replied as she squeezed the trigger, letting off what sounded like an explosion, sending a bullet straight to the man's eye and out the back of his head.

Red then softly grabbed the gun as Latisha turned around and hugged her uncle, whispering the words, "Are you really my uncle?"

"Yes, baby, everything is gonna be alright. But, we're gonna have to leave here and never come back," replied Red.

"What about my mom?" asked Latisha.

"She's not your mom, Latisha, and I promise to explain everything to you later. Now, go and get your stuff and let me take care of Larry," replied Red.

Latisha ran and started packing. She couldn't believe she had just killed a man, but she had no remorse. When she came back out her room, Uncle Red had cleared the blood up, rolled Larry's dead body in a rug, and was carrying it out the door. After a very brief explanation of what was going on, all Latisha left behind was a letter…

Aunt Rose,

I'm leaving and never coming back. Don't try and find me 'cause you won't be able to. Just know I'm safe now. It's time for me to move on and be the Princess that I'm supposed to be...

Love, Princess Tisha

From that day on, Red took care of her and trained her like a hit man. That was why the Reaper was so easy to infiltrate. Red knew once King tried to get out, Agent Fellows would try and kill him using his number one killer. With Latisha's skills it wasn't hard to turn into the Reaper's number one protégée, and now she stood like a little girl arguing with her brothers and looking for her dad's sympathy.

* * * * *

"A'right, a'right, I don't care who did what to who, everybody have a seat and relax, okay? There are some things I want to say," King said as the room became instantly quiet. "I know I haven't been there for y'all as a father, and you may be sitting there with hatred toward me, but I wanna say I'm sorry. I know sorry doesn't get the time back we've lost together, but y'all deserve an apology. Accepting it is up to y'all, and I won't be mad if any of you get up and walk out the door right now." Nobody moved as King paused, and then continued. "I know growing up hasn't been easy, but the stuff we go through in life that doesn't kill us, only makes us stronger. I know your mother would have loved to be here with us right now, and believe me, that's what me and her had planned, but even though she's not here physically, there's no doubt in my mind that she'd want us to keep moving on with the plan," he said while making his way to have a seat with them at the table. He was making eye contact with all of them before he continued. "Today is a special day, it's a day I've dreamed about for a very long time, and now it is here. Today is the day that y'all take over the Royal Family." The kids' eyes got big like they couldn't believe what he was saying, but they said nothing as they listened even closer.

"I know that shit sounds good, but let me tell you, when you're at the top, everybody wants to take your place. You are responsible for not only yourselves, but all of your followers. At no time will you show fear. Once the sharks smell blood, they'll eat you alive!" King said in a loud voice as he slammed his hand to the table, getting his point across. Then, lowering his voice as he continued, he said, "At this moment, the world doesn't know if I'm dead or alive, and that gives us an advantage right now. The police and the Feds are gonna be so busy trying to figure it out, they won't be ready for what we have prepared for them. With that, I'd like to introduce you to our future. It's what I call, The Beast. He took the blue pellet out of his pocket and held it in his hand for them to see. "This little blue pellet is gonna make us billions of dollars, and in the process, change poverty in the hood forever. Those white people that look down upon our people and our hoods, and do their best to keep us in them will now see what it feels like. No longer will the hustlers have to serve crack and heroine to their people to survive. Now, they can shine when they can sell this one pellet for fifty dollars to the white man that's happy to see us kill ourselves day in and day out. We'll supply the three projects. Each project will have a lieutenant that we'll give him The Beast at ten apiece. That will give him plenty money to make sure everyone's eating way more than what they are used to. Anybody that doesn't like that crack and heroine will no longer be sold in our buildings or on our blocks will have to be made an example of in order to let everyone know there will be punishment for their disrespect. Any time there is a hostile takeover, there will be bloodshed and with the move we are making, there is gonna be a lot of unhappy people. One in particular is Benny. He not only controls the projects, he controls the city and he is not gonna just lay down without a fight. He will lie down, that is a promise I'm gonna see to it myself." Then, King started grinning like he couldn't wait to see Benny again. He had plans for him.

"Money brings power and when we affect their money,

you affect their power, and that is what we are going to do. Friday, we're gonna start distribution. First, we're gonna hit all the rave parties in the city, giving out free testers and a phone number if they want some more. That gives you a week to be prepared. Take this time to see who is running what and who is gonna be a problem. Show them your shine and throw a little money around, but don't tell anybody about Friday. With that, the throne is yours. Do you have any questions?"

"No."

"No."

"No," they replied one after each other.

"Good, now that we got the business out of the way, I have something for y'all that I think will help out. So, if you will, follow me next door." King then stood up, gesturing for them to follow him.

The first warehouse had lights on inside. As they made their way to it, Red met them at the door, leading them into a surprise that made the twins' eyes almost pop out their head. In front of them sat two box Chevys with their name on the license plates of each of their cars. The candy yellow Chevy, which read, *Twon* on the plates had the guts done in green and yellow with more green than yellow. The candy green Chevy guts were done with the same colors, except it had more yellow than green. The paint looked like it was wet. The twenty-four inch Lexanis made them sit up like trucks. Even the Chevy tops on the dual exhaust pipes looked like they were just put on. They were soon distracted by the 454 engines under the hood. Inside the car was a PlayStation, two TVs in the headrest, and two twenty inch TVs that fell down from the ceiling. In the front was an Alpine touch screen radio, a little Kenwood EQ that was perfectly mounted where the driver could reach it, and in the trunk was six Rockford Fosgate 15s with four amps as long as the trunk. One amp controlled the six 6x9s and sixteen tweeters inside.

"Well, do y'all like 'em?" King asked.

"Hell yeah," they said at the same time. "Thanks, Pops." Qwon said, with Twon finishing his sentence.

"Don't thank me, thank your sister. She did this for y'all." The twins turned to look at their sister with pride – the same sister that just pointed a gun at them.

"Thanks, Sis. We're, uh, sorry about earlier," Twon said, helping his brother finish what he was trying to say.

"Yeah, yeah, enough with this soft shit. Who gonna give me a ride?" Latisha said, making her way toward Twon's Chevy, thinking to herself that she was gonna like having two little brothers, even if they were crazy as her.

"I guess you riding with me," Twon said, but she had already got in and closed the door.

"Qwon, I put that bag with y'all money in your back seat. One more thing…when y'all get in your car, push y'all hazard light button three times and push the cigarette lighter in," Red said, standing next to King who was looking so proud.

The twins jumped in their cars and followed Uncle Red's

directions, and once they pushed the lighter in, the part above the glove compartment slid out and there were two spaces where their Desert Eagles fit perfectly. There was another surprise, but Red didn't tell them, hoping they would never need it.

"Is y'all gonna sit here all day or is y'all gonna go have some fun?" King yelled to the twins.

They didn't even answer; they just started their new toys, revving the engines as the duals sounded like they were gurgling.

"Twon, give this to Qwon," Latisha said, pulling a cell phone out of her purse and handing it to her brother. "Tell him to follow us," she finished saying before the music drowned her out. The trunk sounded like gorillas were trying to break loose as Twon closed the door and pulled off. 50 Cent sounded like he was in the car with them in concert. *"Many men wish death upon me, blood in my eyes, Lord, and I can't see"*.

In only seconds, King and Red watched as the Chevys took off down the road, knowing now there was no turning back.

* * * * *

Monday 1:00pm

The Marion Jones project was in full swing, even in the brisk weather. It didn't stop the hustlers from getting money.

The word of King's escape or death earlier was still the talk of the projects. The projects were run by a nigga named Goldie. He was a light skin dude that kept a tight fade. He was only five-nine, but nobody crossed him, especially since he worked for Benny. As Goldie made his way out of one of the four buildings that made up the Marion Jones, his gold chain swung as he walked toward his soldiers and workers that turned and quickly greeted him.

"What's happening, boss man?" the dark skinned dude called Slim said. Slim was the man under Goldie.

"What's good, Slim?" Goldie said.

"Shit, money going good, especially with this shit about King in the air. It seems like people done came out of every-where to shop," replied Slim.

"They still ain't found out if he's dead or not?" Goldie said, looking down the street for where that music was coming from.

"Nope, they don't know shit," Slim replied, looking in the same direction as Goldie.

"Who the fuck is beating like that? It sounds like they about four blocks away," Goldie said, looking even harder.

Everybody outside seemed to stop and look as the beating got closer, and was setting off car alarms. The first thing they saw at the stop sign was Twon's yellow Chevy pull up and begin to turn toward the projects. Everyone's head turned the other way as Qwon pulled up to the opposite corner in the green Chevy and turned toward the projects. Both Chevys were coming toward each other until they were directly in front of the projects.

"Shit, them mu'fuckas killin' 'em," Goldie said, trying to see who was driving. Then, the passenger window on Twon's Chevy went down and Goldie walked closer till he saw it was the twins.

"What up, Goldie?" Twon said, turning down the music.

"Damn, niggas, this how y'all doing it?" Goldie replied as he walked around, checking out both cars, making his way to the driver's window. Qwon, let his driver side window down as Goldie stood in the middle and gave both brothers dap.

"How can I be down?" Goldie asked.

"Nigga, get the fuck out of here, all that money you got." Qwon replied. Then, a voice from Twon's passenger seat caught Goldie's attention.

"Aye, we having a party tonight at the Red Light. Why don't you and ya peeps come on through,." Latisha said.

"And, who are you, Ms. Lady?" Goldie asked.

"Maybe you'll find out if you come," replied Latisha.

"I think I might do that," Goldie said.

"Man, we finna be up out of here," Qwon said, getting Goldie's attention back.

"Fa sho', niggas. I'll catch you'll later," Goldie said as he turned and walked back to where his squad was standing.

Qwon then spoke across to Twon and Tish. "How we supposed to get in the Red Light, Tisha?"

"It's easy when you own it," replied Latisha.

"Own it?" Twon said, jumping in the conversation.

"Yeah, we own it. Now, let's get out of here, we got shit to do for tonight," replied Latisha.

"Damn, shit just get better and better," Qwon said as he shifted his Chevy, did a 360 turn in the intersection, and pulled up behind his brother with the music back up. Twon turned his music back up and pulled off with his brother right behind.

"Damn, the twins done came up," Goldie said to Slim.

"What they want?" replied Slim.

"Shit, they having a party at the Red Light and they invited the whole squad," said Goldie.

"So, what you wanna do, boss man?" asked Slim.

"Shit, we about to go shopping. First this shit with King, now they done came through shitting on the town. We most definitely going. They got some serious shit going on and I want a piece. Tell everybody to be ready by eleven, and then grab the whip," Goldie said as he turned and walked away. He couldn't help thinking, *It's gonna be some shit around here, especially if King's alive. He ain't gonna be able to show his face. That puts the twins at the top of the food chain. When the shit goes down, I ain't gonna get left in the cold.*

As the Twins hit the corner, they had one more stop on their list only a couple blocks away. They pulled up on the liquor store and they saw exactly who they were looking for.

"Hey, you fat bitch!" Qwon yelled to the fat nigga on

the corner eating Cheetos. He was wearing a Pelle bomber with a hoody underneath it. The fat nigga turned and looked because it could be no one but two niggas that played with him like that.

"So, that's what y'all niggas on, pull up flossing and insulting a nigga? I told y'all I got an eating disorder."

"Nigga, get you fat ass in and let's ride," Qwon said, letting the window up and watching their nigga, Trouble, making his way around to the passenger door.

Trouble was about six feet and weighed about two hundred and ninety pounds. He may have been a big nigga, but he stayed groomed up and in the freshest gear, plus, a pocket full of money. The twins and Trouble met when the twins moved into the projects. It was about a week after they had moved in they saw four niggas trying to jump Trouble behind the building. Even though they didn't know the fat boy, they jumped in and evened the odds. The boys were about twice their age. Trouble was only a year older than the twins, but when the older niggas seen it was King's twins, they ran off.

"Man, you cold, nigga?" Qwon asked as Twon helped the fat boy up.

"Hell yeah, them niggas wanted me to give up my shit, but I wasn't going to. Good looking out, y'all sho' saved a nigga." From that moment on, they had a bond that only hood niggas could understand. Later on that night, them same niggas that tried to rob Trouble were walking to the store when they were gunned down in the street. Witnesses say they saw three niggas running away with masks on. One kind of fat and the other two with about the same build.

"What the fuck, y'all done robbed a bank?" Trouble asked while getting in the car and looking around as the car pulled off from the curb, following the other Chevy up the block.

"There you go with the questions. A nigga can't have shit nice without a nigga thinking you done took something," replied Qwon.

"You can miss me with that shit, Qwon," Trouble said.

"It's hard to miss your fat ass with anything," replied Qwon.

"Fuck you, nigga," replied Trouble, both of them now laughing.

"Man, but on some serious shit, that shit with your pops got the hood going crazy. That is all people talking about. Dude like an urban legend in the streets," said Trouble.

"I know. We just come through the projects and people was out everywhere. When they seen us, it was like they'd seen a ghost," replied Qwon.

"Niggas know who the streets belong to," said Trouble.

"They better," Qwon said, grinning at his nigga and turning the music up till the vibration had them numb. The only thing they could do was bob their heads.

Twon drove as he followed his sister's directions. After about ten minutes, they were uptown where people with money lived, mostly white though. Uptown and the hood were totally different. It was clean, and there weren't niggas on every corner or dope fiends walking around with baskets and shit.

"Turn here," Tish said, pointing to a street that was taking them along condos with backyards overlooking the lake.

"Damn, look at these cribs," Twon said.

"You like this shit, lil' bro?" replied Latisha.

"Hell yeah," said Twon.

"Well, you see that big white condo on your left with all the windows, Twon?"

"Yeah," replied Twon.

"That's our shit," said Latisha.

"Get the fuck out of here," Twon said.

"Pull in the driveway, stay to the left, though, that's your side of the garage," Tish said.

Tish pulled out a remote that opened all three garage doors. Behind the middle garage door was a Benz—all white with a pink rinse sitting on some twenty-twos, and the license plate read *Tish*.

"Damn, Sis, that's how you doing it?"

"Yeah, I can't let y'all have all the fun," Tish said, giggling.

Twon let down his window and motioned for his brother to let the window down as well. "That is your parking space over there," Twon said, pointing toward the empty space to the far right.

Trouble was in a daze looking at the crib they were pulling in the driveway of. "You see that Benz? Whose shit is that?" Trouble asked.

"I think that is my sister's shit," replied Qwon.

"Your sister?" Trouble responded, surprised.

"Yeah, mu'fucka, my sister. It's a long story," replied Qwon.

Trouble just started laughing. Once the two Chevys parked in the garage, the doors closed behind them and the light came on. Once they were out of the cars, Tish was already headed toward the door to the rest of the house.

"Is y'all gonna stay here or is y'all coming in? Don't forget to grab y'all bag, Qwon," Tish said.

"Oh yeah, I almost forgot that shit was in the car," Qwon replied.

"Damn, twins, that y'all sister?" Trouble said.

"Trouble, don't get fucked up," the twins said at the same time.

"Twon, who crib is this?" Qwon asked.

"Ours, nigga," replied Twon.

They thought the outside of the crib was something, but when they got inside it looked like something out of MTV *Cribs*.

"Come on, y'all, let me show y'all around," Tish said, leading them downstairs first.

The downstairs was like a club. It had a full bar, two big screens, wrap around couch, and two bedrooms. The bathroom was as big as a bedroom. They made their way back upstairs. The living room was huge. It had another big, white wrap around couch, and a sixty-two inch TV. They even had a big screen in the kitchen, but the shit that took their breath away was the whole back of the house. It was made up of windows that looked out at Lake Michigan. Tisha's room was on that floor, the big master suite with pink everything from the bed to the TV. She took them upstairs.

"This floor is y'alls'. I hope y'all like it," Tisha said, leading the way. They had a living room like downstairs, but had video games, lounging sofa chairs, and a Scarface painting on the walls.

"Twon, yours is the first room and, Qwon, that's yours. I left y'all a little gift on your beds.

Y'all ain't gonna introduce me to y'all friend?" she asked.

"That's Fatboy, this is our sister, Tish," Qwon said as he walked toward his room.

"Fuck you, Qwon. My name is Trouble. It's nice to meet you, Tish."

"You, too, Trouble. Qwon so rude," she said, laughing.

The boy's rooms were identical, high ceilings, king sized beds, and walk in closets. The bathroom had a shower and a bath tub. In each of their bathrooms was another door that led to a room in between the twins' rooms that had a big hot tub.

"Oh shit," the boys yelled at the same.

Tish knew they had found their surprise. In the middle of their beds lay a platinum chain that hung easily down to their dicks and at the end of them was the initial of their name, full of crushed diamonds.

"Now that y'all got them big as closets, y'all need to go get some shit to fill them," Tish yelled to them on her way back downstairs.

"Damn, niggas, y'all rich. I ain't never going home," Trouble said just as excited as the twins.

"You ain't got to, nigga, you know we all fat together," Qwon said, with Twon finishing his sentence.

"We gotta get ready for the party tonight," Twon said.

"What party?" Trouble asked.

"Oh yeah, I forgot to tell you we own the Red Light, too," Qwon replied.

"The Red Light? That's the biggest club in the city," Trouble replied, looking surprised.

Qwon grabbed the duffle bag on the couch and unzipped it, grabbed out a stack of money that read twenty thousand, threw it to Trouble, and reached back in and grabbed two more stacks for him and Twon.

"Let's go shopping, ma'fuckas," Qwon said.

Trouble was in shock. He couldn't believe he was holding that much money in his hand.

"Thanks, y'all. Y'all the realist niggas I know," said Trouble.

"And, you the fattest we know. Now, are we gonna stay

here being sentimental or are we gonna go pop some tags?" Qwon asked, zipping the bag up and walking to the stairs with Trouble and Twon right behind.

When they hit the bottom of the stairs, the aroma of Hydro filled the air and on the couch sat Tish with a perfectly rolled backwood full of Dro in her lips burning slow.

"Y'all wanna smoke?" Tish asked.

"Hell yeah," they all said together, making their way to the couch to get in rotation.

"The mall is gone have to wait a while," Twon said, looking at the two other blunts on the table.

"Hell yeah," Qwon said, trying not to cough his lungs up.

Trouble didn't say shit. He was still in shock from all the stuff that had just went on.

"If y'all want some more Dro later, it's some blunts and weed in y'all dresser drawer in y'all rooms," Tish said.

"Do you ever stop?" Qwon said, with Twon finishing his sentence.

"Why, y'all ain't having fun? How about you, Trouble? You having fun?" Tish responded.

"Shit, can y'all adopt me?"

"Hell naw, not as much as you eat," Qwon added, then they all start laughing.

* * * * *

The reporters were still everywhere, still trying to find

out if King was dead or alive, but nobody was allowed to answer. They even tried to ask Agent Fellows as he made his way through the crowd approaching the yellow tape that surrounded the scene, flashing his badge to the offer guarding the tape. The officer quickly lifted the tape, letting Fellows by. He made an observation of the scene as he walked to the command post to get some answers.

"Who is in charge here?" Fellows demanded as he approached.

"I am, Detective Johnson," the stocky detective said.

"Nice to meet you, detective," Fellows said, reaching his hand out to shake hands.

"I'm Agent Fellows, FBI, we're gonna be leading the investigation since Tyler Scott was a federal inmate."

"This is my crime scene, Agent Fellows, we got at least ten police missing right now and I'm not gonna sit back because the FBI wants to chase after an inmate." Johnson said, having to be restrained by his other officers.

"Detective Johnson, I understand your concern, but I'm not asking you, I'm telling you. Now, if you wanna keep your job, I suggest you lose the attitude," Agent Fellows said, turning and pointing at the agents that were approaching. "You see these agents? I expect for them to be filled in on what is going on. Anything that you find out, I wanna be the first to know. Do we understand, Johnson?"

Johnson only nodded his head in agreement, knowing he couldn't win.

"Good. Now that we have that understood, what do we have so far?" Agent Fellows asked Johnson, who had calmed down.

"Nothing, absolutely nothing. The fires have destroyed damn near everything. We found some shell casings next to what we think are bodies. Agent Fellows, I hate to be the rain on your parade, but there is no way possible that you're gonna be able to tell if your inmate is in there or not. With this cold air, it took the firefighters two hours to put the fires out, but from what was left of the transport van, you can see that somebody was shackled," Johnson said.

"How about dental records?" Agent Fellows said, interrupting.

"Ain't no way in hell you gonna get a dental record. Shit, we can't even tell the head from the ass. It's sad to say, but whatever happened here might just stay a mystery. We ain't got no witnesses, no nothing," Johnson replied.

"Thanks, Johnson. Anything else you find out, please, inform my agents," Fellows said as he turned and walked away in frustration while doing his best not to show it.

Fellows knew in his heart that King wasn't dead, but with no proof, there was nothing he could do about it, at least not now. The week had been really fucked up for Fellows. First, he lost two agents that still hadn't been found, King pulled a Houdini ,and The Reaper disappeared off the map. *What's next?* he thought as he popped two Tums before making his way back through the sea of reporters.

* * * * *

The trip to the mall turned into a shopping spree for the twins and Trouble. They went store to store, buying clothes, shoes, and jewelry like they had never had shit. The man at the jewelry store almost hit the panic button when he saw the three hoods come in, but by the time they left he was grinning ear to ear at his new friends that had just spent twenty-five thousand dollars in about fifteen minutes. They bought big diamond earrings for the night, but what cost the most was the matching diamond rings they bought. They even got Latisha one.

Qwon said, "The rings are for the heads of this family."

Trouble didn't know what he was talking about, but he knew he would soon find out. Plus, he was ride or die for the twins since day one, now he was standing in the jewelry store trying his ring on. When they left the mall, they could barely fit all the bags in the car. They had decided to take one car so they could finish smoking the blunt they rolled for the trip to the mall. They could barely squeeze in as they pulled off.

"Man, it's going down tonight," Trouble said.

"Hell yeah, it's going to be bitches everywhere," Twon replied.

"Oh, we most definitely fucking something tonight," Qwon added, and then turned the music up, speeding down the highway on their way back to the house on the lake.

The preparation for the night had to be perfect. It was

about ten p.m. when everybody met in the living room dressed to kill. The twins rocked their matching Pelle fits and finished off with fresh, all white Forces. You couldn't miss the diamonds blinding a nigga at the end of their chains. Trouble had the Akademiks fit, black Akademiks hoody, black Akademik jeans with the black Forces. They were all rockin' diamond earrings. They had to make their ears hurt.

When Latisha hit the room, she had on a little pink skirt, pink Louis Vuitton boots with straps that seemed to climb her thick thighs, her tight shirt showing her belly ring, her hair was honey blond, her Chanel glasses were pink like her outfit, and her lip gloss shined like her diamond bracelet, which was filled with pink diamonds. The ring her brothers and Trouble bought her was hanging like a charm on her platinum chain.

"What you got on?" Qwon said, looking at his sister.

"Clothes, nigga," replied Tish.

"Shit, I can't tell," Qwon said.

"Boy, I am grown," she said, rolling her eyes.

"Don't get fucked up, Tish," Qwon said, with Twon finishing his sentence.

"Let's go. Y'all follow me to the club, haters," Tish said, thinking it was cute her little brothers had bought her the ring as a sign of leadership. That meant they were learning quick, plus, they were protective of her.

The club scene was packed. Everybody that was somebody was in the line to get in. The line was around the block. The niggas flossed the whips up and down the street in front of the club. The twins killed everything out there in the matching Chevys, and Tish's pink Benz for the lookers. Tish pulled right in front of the door, followed by the twins. They hopped out, letting the valet park the cars. While walking toward the door, the twins and Trouble couldn't believe how people were looking at them like they were celebrities. There was no wait for the owners. The big bouncer dropped the velvet rope that blocked off the entrance as soon as they approached.

"This is Tank, y'all. If you have a problem, he'll take care of it," Tish said, introducing the big bouncer on their way in the door. The twins and Trouble gave the big man the nod, and he turned, opening the door for his young bosses.

The boys' eyes grew huge when they stepped in the door. The club had three floors, one dance floor downstairs and a glass dance floor that was built on the third floor overlooking everything. There were so many people, you could barely move. The music bumped Lil John so loud you couldn't hear yourself think. Tish motioned for the boys to follow her, making their way to a stairway that took them up to the office that overlooked everything. When they got to the top of the stairs, there were two bouncers waiting on guard as their bosses approached and passed them on the way to the office.

The office area had a huge balcony that allowed them to see everything and next to the office was a private area to kick it just for them. Once in the office, the boys were amazed at how the music disappeared once they closed the door. They did not know they were surrounded by sound proof glass. The office was huge, they had their own bar, and TVs were everywhere. There were big reclining sofas and on the wall was a picture of King and Queen.

"Damn this shit like a crib," Qwon said, looking around.

"Hell, this that top of the world shit right here," Twon added.

"Well, this is how we do it. If y'all go out there and look off the balcony and you see something you like, tell the bouncers and they'll go get it for you," Tish told the boys while pouring Remy in there glasses. The boys wasted no time going out to the balcony with their glasses in their hands, just staring down at the crowd of people.

"Y'all have fun. I got some things to handle," Tish said, exiting through a back route with a bouncer close behind her.

The boys pointed out female after female. They even saw they nigga, Goldie, in the sea of people, and before you knew it, in the VIP Room was Goldie, Trouble, and twins, and they partied like rock stars with at least ten females, some that were naked and on their knees giving head like it was a game and they had to win.

"Man, I can believe y'all own this shit," Goldie said, taking a hit from the Kush that was rolled in his blunt. "But, y'all sho' showing a nigga some love," he said, looking at the naked red bone walking in front of him.

"Don't even trip, nigga. It's gonna get greater, just stick with us," Qwon replied, taking a swig out of the Remy bottle.

"Goldie, you know you our nigga, plus, you always looked out for us," Twon added, taking the blunt Goldie passed him.

"Shit, me and the squad riding with y'all, just show us which way to go and we there."

"Fa sho'," Qwon replied as he turned his head to see Trouble coming out of the bathroom with two bitches by his side.

"Damn, y'all just having too much fun without me," Tish said, entering the VIP, but she wasn't alone. She was followed by about five of the baddest bitches the twins, Goldie, and Trouble had ever seen.

"Damn, Sis, where you get them from?" Qwon asked, getting up and passing his sister the Remy bottle.

"They said they wanted to meet y'all. Except for this one, she wanted to meet me," she said, referring the thick, caramel skinned female that looked like she just came out of a video.

"Get y'all another bottle, I'm taking this one with me," Tish said, leading the caramel skinned female she called "Juicy" into the bathroom and shutting the door. Within minutes, Tish was sitting on the sink hitting the Remy while Juicy had her face deep in Tish's pussy.

"Who is that, nigga?" Goldie asked.

"That's our sister," the twins said at the same time.

The Twins couldn't help but think to themselves, *Damn, our sister loves bitches like us.* The thought quickly left as the new females their sister brought started stripping for them. After about thirty minutes, Tish emerged from the bathroom followed by Juicy.

"Y'all, we got something to do, so tell all your girlfriends you'll see them later," said Tish. The females left quick, only leaving Tish, the twins, Trouble, and Goldie

"Fuck them hoes," Tish said, hitting the blunt Trouble passed her before continuing.

"Wait until you see the ones at our after party tonight," Tish continued.

"I got something planned." They made their way out on the balcony overlooking the club, and at that time you could see waiters making their way through the sea of people passing out glasses of Cristal to everyone. Then, the music stopped and all the attention went toward the balcony where they were standing holding their glasses. Tish had a microphone in her hand, and the radio station that was broadcasting live in the club kept the live feed as Tish began to talk.

"First of all, we would like to thank y'all for coming out tonight. This is a special night for my brothers and me. Tonight, we'd like to have a toast with y'all, so would y'all please raise your glasses?" She paused as everybody held up their glasses. "I would like to toast to our mother and father, King and Queen, and where ever they may be together." Then, they all toasted, and everyone begin applauding and chanting, 'King and Queen,' until they were just as loud as the music.

The radio jockey let it be heard across the radio waves, and then he added, "Long Live the King and Queen," before letting the music take over.

Goldie stood with them on the balcony, knowing he had made his decision, no question. The twins and Trouble felt the power of leadership looking on to their followers' chant. Then, Tish told the DJ crank that shit back up and within seconds, the club was going crazy again. The club rocked to three a.m. Afterwards, it was still like a car show. Security cleared the way for the Chevys and Benz to slide through the after club traffic. While leaving, they were followed by a white stretch Hummer that was full with at least twenty females ready for the after party activities. The stage was set. Goldie, who was now riding with Twon, was on their team, and the toast at the club was really an introduction of who was in control of the throne.

Part Three

Nation Business

The medical examiner's report hit Agent Fellow's desk like a ton of bricks. King had been ruled dead, along with eight swat team members, two transport officers, three unidentified bodies, and two U.S. Marshals. It was the largest tragedy the city had seen years, and the worst part was that nobody had a clue on what had happened. All they could come up with was it had to be an assassination. Agent Fellows slammed his fist into the desk, knocking his coffee over.

"Bullshit!" he yelled, knowing that the medical examiner had ruled King dead.

There would be no search or further investigation into the matter. All he could do was sit back and wait, but he didn't know what he was waiting on. But, he'd know it when he seen it. He just hoped it wouldn't be too late. He had it made up in his mind. If King showed his face, he would kill 'em himself, no questions asked. It was the second time King had slipped through his hands, and there wouldn't be a third.

* * * * *

January 14 –

Only fifteen days after Queen was laid to rest, King's closed casket sat in the same spot Queen's sat in. Tish and the twins took their seats up front as people poured in from everywhere to pay their respects. The streets outside the church were covered for six blocks with people that chanted, "Long live the King." Even though King started out just selling drugs out of the Marion Jones Projects, he was the people's hope of a new day.

Before he was locked up, he had realized the damage selling drugs to his own people was doing to them, and was trying to correct the problem he was a part of. He paid for drug programs that people in poverty couldn't afford. He built centers for the homeless. He gave out food to the hungry and toys to the kids. The more he did for people, the more people followed him. He never turned his back on anybody, and it showed by all the people that came to the funeral. Although he was supposed to be dead, the people's hope wouldn't let them believe it.

The twins and Tish were rushed by reporters when they

tried to leave the church. "Is the King really dead?"

"Do you know who killed your father?"

"Are you taking off where your father left off?" the reports shouted.

But, they got no response as King's kids jumped into their limo and shut the door. The shouts of, "Long live the king!" shook the limo as it pulled off from the curb. Waiting inside the limo was Uncle Red. "Y'all enjoy the funeral?" Red said, then started laughing.

"For Pops to have been locked away for ten years, I can't tell by all these people," Twon said, looking at his uncle.

"Y'all father owns half this city still, even after ten years. "Those projects y'all lived in, who you think own them?" Uncle Red said, pausing to light a Newport. "Twins, have you ever seen your momma pay rent?" When they thought about it, they hadn't. They just shook their heads no as Red continued. "Even better, I got one more question before we get to business. Have you ever seen your mom get high?" That question threw the boys for a loop. Red could tell by the expression on their face that he wasn't waiting for an answer, because he already knew it. "Now, to business. Tomorrow is the day, are y'all ready?"

"Yeah," Qwon spoke up for them.

"We got the Jones on lock, but Benny got a strong hold on the other two. They ain't gonna come easy," Qwon said.

"Don't worry about them two or Benny. Right now, we gonna flood the Jones. Everything else will fall in place, especially when we hit Benny's connect," Uncle Red said.

"Who's his connect?" Twon asked.

"They call him the Bull. He used to supply your father until your father told him he was getting out the game. Benny and Agent Fellows had been trying to double cross your father and when he went to jail, it was a whole lot easier. The Bull wasted no time dealing with Benny. He didn't want to lose the money your father was making him. When I say money, I don't mean any little shit. I'm talking two hundred to three hundred keys every two weeks type shit. That right there supplies the whole city. But, that was years ago. Benny is probably getting more than that. We only dealt with cocaine. Benny is dealing cocaine and heroin. But, don't trip, when we hit the Bull, he'll never see it coming. The city ain't gonna have shit left. Once we make this hit, then we take the other projects," Red finished while reaching in his pocket and taking out a piece of paper. "This is the name of four clubs and two raves happening tomorrow. Next to each one is a contact person. All y'all gotta do is drop one thousand packs," Red said while showing them the bags of little blue pellets. "They will take care of the rest. They already got the cell phone number to pass out. This is important, though, once you get the business running to the Jones, it's gonna have to be a very tight operation. Sit down with Goldie and y'all work it out. But, the main rule is, under no circumstances is anybody to try this shit or sell this shit to a black person. Y'all understand?"

"Yeah," they all said together, knowing Uncle Red meant business.

"A violation of the rules will not be tolerated and its punishment will be death," Red said as the limo pulled up to the burial grounds. "Now, get y'all ass out and go bury y'all father," he said, then start laughing.

"You always talking shit, Unk," Qwon replied before climbing out and getting kicked in his ass by his uncle.

* * * * *

Following the burial services of King, the twins and Tish knew it was time to get down to business. Tish handled the deliveries of The Beast to the names on the list Uncle Red gave them. In the meantime, the twins sat down with Trouble and Goldie, and let them know what was going down. Within an hour, Trouble, Goldie, and the twins were sitting in the office of the Red Light.

"I know y'all been wondering what's going down lately, but it wasn't time to tell y'all until now," Qwon said, knowing he'd told Trouble the business three days ago. Trouble pretended he was finding out for the first time as Qwon continued. "Goldie, you always been our nigga and I know you getting money, but how about if I told you right now I can turn them thousands you making into millions?"

"Shit, I'd say show me the money, nigga," Goldie replied sitting up in his chair and becoming very interested in what was being said.

"Well, peep this shit out here, nigga. What I'm about to tell you might sound crazy at first, but believe me, the only thing that will be crazy is you if you don't believe what I'm about to tell you. First of all, that shit being sold in the Jones gotta stop. I mean, not slow down, but shut down completely," Qwon continued.

"Shut down, what the fu…" Goldie started saying before he was cut off by Twon getting in the conversation.

"Be easy, nigga. I know that shit sound crazy, but what we about to lie down, nigga, gonna change the hustle. Seeing that we'll be the only ones with it, we gonna get all the money," Twon said.

"What's this shit y'all talking about? Y'all act like y'all got some super hustle. Quit playing and put it in the air," Goldie said, calming down. Qwon reached in his pocket and rolled a little blue pellet across the table to Goldie.

Goldie picked it up and examined it. "What the fuck is this, some X?" Goldie asked.

"Hell naw, nigga, this is the future for the hood, that's what it is. That bullshit we selling in the hood now ain't doing nothing but killing our people off and taking food off our own table. But, that shit you got right there in your hand, nigga, gonna take off them white folk's tables," Qwon said, looking at Goldie for a reaction.

"Yeah?"

"Yeah, nigga," Qwon continued, knowing he had Goldie's attention.

Goldie thought for a second before asking some more questions. "So, you telling me this is gonna replace crack and heroine? But, what about all the customers I got? What they gonna do? I mean, if we take all that shit out the Jones, it's still gonna be in the hood," Goldie said.

"Look, nigga, if we lay this down in the Jones right, we gonna be the hood," Twon finished, waiting on what Goldie had to say next.

"I mean, niggas, if you say this is what it is, put me on the team. All I want to know is where we gonna get the new customers from?" asked Goldie.

"We got that under control. By Saturday night, this shit gonna be running so hard you ain't gonna know what to do. All you gonna have to do is answer this phone," Twon said, sliding the phone across the table to Goldie. "Guide the traffic in, but for no reason is this shit to be sold to any black person or is nobody to use it. If they violate those laws, they will be dealt with. Take that sample and find one of your white clucks to try it. All he gotta do is sit it on his tongue and it will do the rest. We gonna have to change the operation down there 'cause once the police get an idea of what's going on, they gonna be at us, but by then it will be too late. We'll talk prices tomorrow. Do you have any more questions?" Twon said.

"Just one, what's it called?" asked Goldie.

"The Beast," the twins said simultaneously.

"The Beast, yeah, I like that," Goldie replied.

"Trouble, you got that?" Qwon asked.

"Yeah," he replied, passing a little box to Goldie. Goldie opened it and noticed it was the same ring they all had on.

"Put it on, nigga," Qwon said.

"Welcome to the family," the twins and Trouble said, standing up to shake Goldie's hand. Goldie knew there was no turning back. Benny was gonna be pissed, but fuck Benny he thought as he laughed to himself, shaking the hands of his new family.

* * * * *

Goldie's mind was going a million different places as his Cadillac truck pulled up in front of the four massive buildings full of poverty stricken families that made up the Marion Jones. It was the biggest out of the three projects with only a few blocks separating them. There was always competition. The Victoria Projects was only three buildings. They were run by Big Block and the Seventeenth Street boys. Them niggas were real hustlers and stuck to the code M.O.B., money over bullshit. Big Block always said it was hard to make money when you were at war, so they always tried to keep shit cool. As for the Broadway Projects, they were the smallest with only two buildings, but it was like they lived B.O.M., bullshit over money. The head nigga out there was a nigga named Blow, and that nigga was on some shoot first, ask questions never shit.

Since Goldie was getting out the competition, he

wondered how that was gonna change shit around there. Could that little ass pellet change everything? He didn't know, but it was time to find out. Goldie was getting out of his truck as Slim approached to greet him. Slim's eyes went straight to the huge diamond ring on Goldie's hand before he start talking.

"What up, Goldie? Where you been shopping, nigga? That ring blinding a nigga."

"Naw nigga, it's a gift and in a minute, we gonna have a lot of gifts around here," replied Goldie.

"What you talking 'bout, Goldie?" Slim asked.

"I'm gonna tell you, but first round up the squad. I mean all of them, no exceptions. It's sixty-five of us on count and sixty-five niggas better be in the courtyard in an hour. You got it?" Goldie said, walking away toward the buildings.

"Fa sho. I'm on it, nigga," replied Slim.

"One more thing," Goldie said, turning back toward Slim. "Find Andy white ass and bring him, too."

"Andy?" Slim replied, looking confused.

"Yeah, Andy. You'll understand later, nigga, just do it," Goldie said as he turned back and walked off, knowing that shit better work or he was gonna look like a fool in front of the squad. When you were the head, you had no room for fuck ups.

Even though the weather was chilly, the squad started assembling quick and with only forty-five minutes from the time Goldie's order was made, there was the sixty-five squad members, including Andy's white ass.

The Squad was standing in front of their leader, who was standing on an old picnic table so he could be seen.

"A'ight, a'ight, everybody, be easy," Goldie said, motioning his hands for everybody to be quiet. Within seconds, you couldn't hear a whisper. Then, he continued. "I know it's cold out here, but this ain't gonna take long, so pay attention 'cause I'm only gonna say this shit once. There's gonna be some changes around here in the next couple of days that y'all might think sounds crazy right now, but if you trust me, you'll see so much paper you won't have nowhere to hide it all." The crowd started mumbling, but Goldie continued. "Today, the squad is going into a new business. We ain't selling work and diesel no more." He paused as the mumbles really got loud until he had to motion for them to be quiet again, knowing it was the moment of truth. "I know y'all like, 'What the fuck, Goldie,' but I'm gonna show you what I'm on," Goldie said while reaching in his pocket and pulling out the sample of The Beast the twins had gave him earlier. "I know all y'all can't see, but this little ass blue pellet is the future for the squad. They call this The Beast, and we the only ones with it." The crowd was really restless, looking at Goldie like he had lost his fucking mind. Goldie knew it was now or never as he waved for Andy to come forward. He hoped in the back of his mind that shit was what the twins said it was. Andy came forward and stood up on the picnic table next to Goldie, wondering what the fuck was going on.

"A'right, everybody, shut the fuck up!" Goldie said. Even though the squad was getting restless and aggravated with what they had just heard and their leader had just laid down on them, they knew Goldie was not to be played with. When he said shut the fuck up, he meant shut the fuck up and that was what they did instantly. "Y'all think I'd stand out here in the cold ass weather to make a fucking fool out of myself? I ain't never steered the squad wrong, and I ain't about to start now. Even better, peep this shit."

Turning toward Andy, he knew the moment of truth had arrived. "Andy, take this and put is on your tongue."

"What's in it?" Andy asked.

"Quit asking fucking questions, mu'fucka. Do you wanna get high or what?" replied Goldie. Even though it sounded like a question Andy knew it was a command, and placed The Beast on his tongue instead of asking anymore questions that would probably get him fucked up without a doubt. The squad paid close attention, right along with Goldie, who didn't know what to expect no more than they did. Within seconds, Andy's eyes seemed to be the size of silver dollars as The Beast took over his body. He had never been so high so quick.

All he could say was, "Oh shit." He was so high, Goldie had to grab Andy before he fell off the table.

"Andy, you good?" Goldie asked, knowing he had surely got the squad's attention by the silence that seemed to be a quiet over them.

"Am I good? Fuck good. I ain't ever felt like this

before, I'm so fucking high. What the fuck, man, this shit is incredible," Andy replied.

With that, Goldie knew he'd proved his point as he stood back up after helping Andy take a seat.

"You see that shit?" Goldie paused, talking with confidence. "That shit there gonna make us rich. Fuck Benny." He got us out here selling that other shit to our moms, aunts, and uncles, getting money by taking out of each other's mouths. Well, it ain't happening no more. This shit here is only to be sold to white people, and for no reason will any of you try this shit. Do you understand me?"

"Yeah," everyone seemed to yell all together like real soldiers.

"Royalty is back in the Jones. The twins and their sister, Tish, are taking over the throne, and they've belled me into the Royal family," Goldie said while holding up his ring as he continued. "And, that means the Squad is now Royalty. If anybody wants to leave, then leave now 'cause once this moment is gone, there won't be a second chance to leave," Goldie said as he paused, waiting to see if anybody wanted to leave. Nobody budged. They stood there like a football team in the locker room of a championship game getting a pep talk from their coach. "I see nobody wants to leave. It's ride or die from here on out. Saturday, we kick this shit off and selling this shit here. We gonna have to step our games up 'cause it's gonna get real hot around here, but if we do this shit right, they'll stop our money. I don't want a word of this to leak out to nobody. Not your bitch, not anybody, 'cause believe me, we will find out who the leak is." Goldie paused and gave that look to his followers like that shit was serious enough to die for.

"Now, get all the shit we got left together and sell it half price, and whatever we got left Saturday, we getting rid of it. We in Beast mode now, niggas."

Goldie looked down at Andy, who was sitting there in a zone. Still only saying, "I'm so fucking high."

Goldie started laughing, then looked back at the squad, giving them his final command. "Let's get it." Then, he stepped down, putting his hood on, and then putting his hand in his Pelle coat pockets before walking off with Slim.

The Squad dispersed, walking past Andy who was still saying, "I'm so fucking high." They laughed and joked, but they knew shit was about to go down. Benny wasn't gonna like what was going down, but if he wanted a war, he'd better know those niggas lived S.O.E. Squad over Everything.

* * * * *

Friday night went smooth. All the drops were made to the connects Uncle Red had gave them, except for the last one. Tish was gonna do it alone. Her Benz ended up filled with the twins and Trouble. She couldn't blame them, they were curious just like her. They wanted to see The Beast in action. The plan was to hang around the last rave party and see for themselves, and that was what they did.

The connect's name was Flip. He was a light-skinned black dude, about six-two, and maybe a buck sixty soaking with an afro. He motioned for them to follow him toward the back. They made their way through the crowd as the Techno music seemed to have everybody in a trance. Trouble could have sworn he saw somebody fucking on the floor, but they kept moving till they were in a back office.

"Damn, these mu'fuckas is kicking it," Qwon said, bouncing his head to the beat that was shaking the office walls.

"It's still early," Flip said in his deep voice as he reached out and took the package Tish handed him.

Flipped carefully looked at it and said, "Well, this is The Beast shit. I wanna see what this shit can do."

"We do, too," Tish said.

"Fuck it, let's put this shit out there. Why wait?" Flip said, opening the door and waving to a little white boy with a book bag on. When he came running, Flip handed him the package, whispered something to him, and turned back around.

"Come on, y'all, we going upstairs and have a couple of drinks and watch this shit," Flip said.

"After you," Tish said as they followed Flip to the upper level where they could see everything while they sipped Remy with Flip.

"Y'all want some of these," Flip said, yelling over the music while he held up a sandwich bag that looked like it had different color candies in it.

"What's that?" Twon asked.

"Ecstasy," Flip replied.

"Yeah, how much that shit cost?" Twon asked.

"Free for y'all," Flip replied, tossing the bag of fifty pills to Twon.

"Y'all pop one of them and get some bitches. I guarantee it will be a night you won't forget," Flip said.

"Fuck that, let me get one now," Tish said, snatching the bag from her brother.

They knew they would party because the next day it was time for business. They all took a pill out of the bag and took them at the same time since that was their first time popping. Flip waved for a female to bring bottled waters for them, knowing they would sure need them soon. In the meantime, Qwon lit up the Kush he had rolled in a backwood and began the smoke session while they waited. Flip was hitting the blunt when he pointed toward his little white boy with the book bag who was across the other side of the party at the DJ table whispering something to the DJ.

"It's about to go down," Flip said, blowing Kush smoke in the air.

"A'ight, everybody," the Asian DJ started saying across the mic. "We got some new shit in the house called The Beast. We got free testers coming around. All you gotta do is sit it on your tongue and let it do the rest. Now, let's get this shit back cranking," he finished, turning the music back up. Within minutes, the white boy with the book bag was making his way through the crowd, giving out testers of The Beast with a number to call. In the rave, they wasted no time taking free drugs. One by one, they popped the little pellet on their tongues, not knowing that its effects would be immediate.

"You see that shit," Qwon said, pointing toward the first area The Beast was passed out in.

The whole section seemed to be on a whole nother level. Their eyes, their movements were changed in a matter of seconds, and the music seemed to feed them. It was like a wave as section after section of the club was ate up by The Beast. Some were so high they were just stuck with nothing but their head bouncing. Others rubbed their face, well, what they thought was their face, considering they could not feel it.

"I ain't never seen no shit like this before in my life," Flip said, standing with his mouth wide open in amazement. Forgetting he was holding the blunt, not trying to pass it, the twins, Tish, and Trouble couldn't believe the power of The Beast as they stood there shaking their heads.

"My bad, Flip," Qwon said, taking the blunt from Flip's extended arm that had been holding the blunt out for the last minute. He did not know the fire had gone out.

"That shit there is gonna take over everything," Flip said.

The DJ came back on the mic "What y'all think about The Beast out there?" The people screamed so loud it shook the building. It was like they were at a rock concert. "The Beast is definitely in the building," the Asian DJ continued as he turned the music up. The rave seemed to go crazy.

"Well, Flip, we'd love to stay longer, but it's time for us to go find some bitches," Tish said while starting to feel the effects of the pill she popped.

"Fa sho, yall, believe me, I understand. Make sure y'all fuck some for me," Flip replied.

"Oh, we will," Tish said, making her way down the stairs with the twins and Trouble right behind her. They didn't say anything until they got in the car and Tish had pulled off.

"That shit was crazy," Qwon said.

"Hell yeah, shit about to get real once this shit drop tomorrow," Trouble added, wiping the sweat from his face. He wondered why he was gritting his teeth. Tish was on the phone with Juicy.

"Where y'all at? How many of y'all is it? Eight? That ain't enough, make them calls and meet us at the house," she said, and then hung up.

"Twon, call Goldie, tell him meet us at the crib. It's going down," Tish said, and then she took a swig of her water.

Within thirty minutes, it was at least fifteen to twenty bad bitches in the house on the lake. And, just like Tish said, it went down.

* * * * *

Goldie's phone woke him early Saturday morning. He

was pulling himself from in between the three bitches he shared the bed with at the twins' crib.

"What up?" Goldie said.

"I know its early, nigga, but this phone you gave me to answer been going crazy," Slim said.

"A'ight, stall them, let me get shit together now. In the meantime, gather up what's left of that and let niggas know that shit dead as of right now. A'ight?" Goldie replied.

"A'ight, Squad," Slim said.

"Squad," was Goldie's last words before ending the call, putting on his pants, and heading up to the twins' room. For it to be six-thirty in the morning, he couldn't believe how woke he was. He figured it was that ecstasy he had popped the night before. As he made his way up the stairs, he could hear that he wasn't the only one still feeling the effects.

"Damn, y'all niggas wide the fuck awake," Goldie said to the twins and Trouble, who were up having a smoke session while sitting on the upstairs couches with the females they had chosen.

"Shit, nigga, what you doing, sleep walking?" Trouble said, passing Goldie the blunt.

"Fuck, nigga," Goldie replied before inhaling the weed smoke into his chest and exhaling. "Man, Slim called me and woke me up. He said we got a green light," Goldie said.

"Damn, already?" Qwon said, tapping Twon on the leg. "Go get Tish up."

"Well, ladies, we've had a good time, but it's time for

y'all to go," Qwon finished while standing up, watching Twon go downstairs to get Tish.

"Tish, Tish," Twon yelled through her bedroom door.

"Come in, nigga, quit yelling like you crazy," Tish replied as Twon opened her room door. His eyes got big as hell when he seen the three females in the bed eating each other out and never even stopping as he came in. Tish was sitting in a chair watching while she rolled a blunt.

"What's good, lil' Bro?" Tish asked as she continued filling her blunt with weed.

"Shiit, this is what's good," he said, pausing to take a second look before he remembered why he was there.

"Oh, oh yeah, it's a green light on that."

"For real?" she asked.

"Well, can you keep them company while I go make a few calls?"

"Hell yeah, Sis, I gotcha," Twon replied, looking back at the females in the bed.

"Oh, Juicy, this my lil' brother. Y'all play nice with him, okay?" Tish said.

One of the females pulled her face from in between a brown skin female's legs and got up and grabbed Twon by his pants, pulling him over in the bed to join in the fun. Tish laughed while standing up with her rolled blunt in her lips. She grabbed her sweat pants and pulled them up over her little pajama shorts and creamy thick thighs on her way out of the room to call Uncle Red.

Red arrived at the house about nine thirty, and everyone was gone except for Trouble, the twins, and Tish. Goldie had gone down to the Jones to get stuff in order. Red come in through the garage with two big duffle bags in his massive hands.

"Y'all ready or what?" he said, dropping the two bags on the floor.

"We've been ready, Unk, quit playing," Qwon replied.

"Shut up, chump, and come get these bags," Red replied.

Trouble couldn't help but laugh at Qwon, who was making his way over to get the bags.

"Ain't shit funny, fat boy," Qwon turned around and said to Trouble.

"Just go get them bags like your uncle said before he fuck you up," Trouble replied.

Qwon couldn't help but laugh at himself.

"There is one hundred thousand pellets in each bag," Red started explaining, walking over toward the couch and taking the blunt from Tish before he continued. "Now the prices," Red said, pausing to hit the blunt. "Y'all bring me back five dollars apiece. Y'all supply the Jones at twenty-five dollars apiece and tell Goldie to put them on the street for fifty dollars apiece. Bottom line is, out of these two bags is a million for me, four million for y'all to split, and four million for Goldie and the Jones. "Got it?"

"Yeah," they said at the same time.

"Good," Red said, getting up and passing the blunt after

taking another hit.

"I sure didn't wanna have to fuck y'all up," he said, grinning to show the edges of his gold teeth. Then, he turned and walked out the same door he came in.

"Trouble, call Goldie and tell him be ready. We'll be there in a minute," Qwon said before running up stairs to get his car keys.

* * * * *

Goldie and Slim were going over the new operation when Trouble called. "Fa sho, nigga," Goldie said into his cell phone before hitting the end button. "It's on its way," Goldie said to Slim.

"Niggas, get ready to get money. Watching all that other money have to go down to the other projects is crazy," Slim replied.

"I know, Slim, but don't even trip. Nigga, we about to get rich for real, so long as we stick to the operation," Goldie said.

The operation they had come up with was one that would surely go down in hustling history. They didn't leave a corner unturned from security, walkie-talkies, scanners, and cameras. They even had their form of background check. Everyone that made a purchase would have to have an I.D. The first time they came, that I.D. would be scanned in a computer. When they had all their information, individuals from the squad would go out to where those people lived and take pictures of their family, their car, and even their dog. Once the client came back to purchase again, they would show them the photos, just in case they ever thought about talking to the police. Even the transaction process was on another level. The client would have to take a certain route to get to the Jones. Along that route, about four to five blocks away they would meet their first contact. The first contact's job was to get their name and number. That number was a special number given to each client in order to recognize them. The second contact was only about two more blocks away. By the time they got to the second contact, their information and photo was on a computer screen waiting on the second contact to take the client's picture with a camera phone and send the picture back to the squad member sitting in front of the computer. By the time the client got to the Jones, the client was either flagged to pull in the parking lot, or given a sign that meant you had to wait, which meant you would have to go through the process all over again or you flat out got ignored, which meant your name, number, or photo wasn't right. If the client was flagged in the parking lot, the client would then be greeted by the fourth contact. His job was to take the client's order and tell him what building to go to. The client would then go to one of the four buildings where they'd be frisked, and then asked for the money by the fifth contact. Once the contact had the money, he would send the client to another building to meet his sixth contact, who would again frisk the client, and then put the client on the elevator and send the client to a specific floor. When the elevator doors opened on the floor, a masked squad member would hand them the product and the client was sent on their way. The floor where the product was would change every two hours, making it impossible to keep up with even the money. Once it was collected in one building, within minutes it was sent to another building. It was a lot of work, but Goldie knew it was necessary to protect them. It was a twenty-four hour a day operation, three shifts like a real job, except the pay would be way more than they could have possibly imagined at that moment.

* * * * *

Within twenty minutes after Trouble made the phone call to Goldie, the twins and Trouble were in the apartment. Goldie posted up with the two big duffle bags full of The Beast that Uncle Red had brought them. After discussing the prices, Goldie couldn't believe that he would be making millions. He would've loved to stay and kick it, but Goldie had his game face on, and it was time for him to do what he did best—get money.

Now that Goldie had the operation under way, the twins and Trouble had some stops to make. Trouble was going to drop a couple dollars on his mama since he hadn't been home since the twins picked him up that day. The twins, on the other hand, were headed back to their old apartment. They had some questions in their head that needed answering, and one question in particular. Had they ever seen their momma use drugs? The question had stuck with them ever since Uncle Red had thrown it at them. Even though they actually couldn't remember, it had to be something in the apartment that would help them.

Their apartment was only a couple floors up from where they had just met Goldie. Within five minutes, they were at the door to the apartment. A soft, nervous feeling came over them as Twon put the key in the lock and opened up the door again for the first time since they'd found their mom dead on Christmas day. They prepared themselves for the stench in the air that death always seemed to leave behind, but to their disbelief, the air only smelled like old Newports like it did when they left.

"What we looking for?" Qwon asked his brother while turning on the light.

"Shit I don't know, but we'll know if we find it," Twon replied.

"You always got some stupid ass answer," Qwon said.

"Fuck you. All I know is most heroin addicts keep a kit somewhere full of their tools," Twon said.

"Why the fuck you still talking, let's go find it," Qwon said, pushing their mom's bedroom door open and turning on the light. Everything was still the same as the day they found her. "Let's get this shit over with," Qwon said.

"I'm with you," Twon replied, getting on his knees to look under the bed while Qwon made his way to the closet to begin his search.

The search lasted for ten minutes and they still hadn't found anything. "Man, this some bullshit," Qwon said, closing the dresser drawers he was looking in.

"Yeah, you right," Twon replied, pulling himself from under the bed. "There's got be something, Bro," Twon continued, standing up and walking around the bed to where their mama was laying when they found her. Twon looked like he had an idea. He bent down and went through her garbage.

"What the fuck are you doing?" Qwon asked with a confused expression on his face as he watched his brother go through the garbage.

"Look, Qwon, here go the wrapper to the needle she used."

"So what?" Qwon replied.

"So what? You slow as fuck sometimes. That means the needle she used was brand new. Why she get a brand new needle to die with?" Twon responded.

"Yeah, that do sound crazy," Qwon replied as he watched his brother pull what looked like a ball of tissue out of the garbage.

"What's that?" Qwon asked while watching his brother unravel the tissue and hold a little jar with a label around it.

"I don't know, it says Ketamine, and it's empty. Look at the top, Qwon," Twon said, turning to show it to his brother.

"That's a needle hole," Twon finished.

"What the fuck is going on?" Qwon said, really looking confused. "We ain't found no foil, no spoon, no nothing, but we find this shit. What is that shit?" Qwon said.

"I don't know, Qwon, but I do know they said momma died from a heroin overdose, and this sho ain't heroine."

Then, a voice from the other room startled them. "Twins, what is y'all doing?"

Twon stuffed the little jar in his pocket and stood up, whispering to his brother, "We'll figure this shit out later."

"Damn, we coming," Qwon yelled to Trouble, who was in the living room.

"We most definitely will figure this out later. Let's ride, nigga" Qwon said to Twon. When the twins left the room, they saw Trouble standing there eating a ninety-nine cent back of Cheetos.

"Why y'all be taking all day?" Trouble asked, licking the cheese off his thumb and index finger.

"Why you be eating all day?" Qwon replied as they exited the apartment. They said twins shared thoughts, and that time they were right because all they both could think was, *What the fuck is going on!*

Part Four

Game Over

O ver the next two weeks, Goldie watched the money pile up. The money counters seemed to never stop counting out thousand after thousand. Twenty-four hours a day, seven days a week, the squad ran the operation to perfection. There was no room for mistakes. It was a whole different ball game than selling rocks and blow. You would make twenty to forty stacks a week off your own people. Now, they were selling to nothing but white people, and that twenty to forty stacks had turned into five million dollars in two weeks. Since the first customer, it seemed like a dream to Goldie. Even having a limit of ten they could buy at a time, the money never stopped coming. The Beast was truly living up to its name, and the twins, Tish, and Trouble were witnessing its power, especially since Goldie had brought five duffle bags to the house on the lake containing one million dollars apiece.

"Damn, nigga, it ain't been but two weeks," Qwon said to Goldie as he unzipped the bags.

"I know, this shit running so hard. I ain't never seen nothing like this in my life. Not even on *New Jack City*. Shit, fuck the Cartel, the Jones is going down in history," Goldie replied.

"What the police been like?" Tish said, getting into the conversation.

"Fuck the police, they too busy worried about the rocks and blows that is booming at the other two projects now that we out of the game. The couple of units that do post up for a few minutes ain't on shit. We know they coming six blocks away," Goldie replied.

"What about Benny?" Tish asked.

"He been making threats, talking about The Jones is his and we ain't got a choice. Like I told him, all he gotta do is come down here and we'll show him how many choices we got," Goldie said.

"Don't worry about him," Tish said, lighting her backwood and taking a pull before finishing what she was saying. "You think he mad now," she continued while pausing to exhale the smoke. "He gonna to be pissed when we hit the shipment coming in this weekend that supplies the city."

"Y'all are talking about fucking with the Bull, the Cartel, and Benny all at one time? That's some gangsta ass, suicidal, ready for war ass shit," Goldie replied while taking a swig from the fifth of Remy Trouble had passed him.

"So, is you down?" Twon said from the kitchen where he was breaking up more weed to roll up on the counter.

"Nigga, am I down?" Goldie said, standing there with his 'nigga what' face on.

"Hell yeah, I wouldn't miss that shit for nothing in the world. Just tell me what you want me to do and it's done," Goldie continued.

"Fa sho, nigga. You had me worried for a minute there," Qwon said.

"Quit playing. You see this big ass diamond ring on my finger? I'm ride or die for my family," Goldie said, holding out his hand with his ring on it that only the five of them had.

"We got a lot of work ahead of us for Sunday night. That leaves two and a half days to come up with a plan," Tish said, getting up to go get the folder full of photos of the operation and their targets. She didn't know how Uncle Red got so much info, but she was happy he was on their side.

* * * * *

Sunday night at ten thirty-five, the loading docks were quiet except for the sixty armed men The Bull had with him waiting on his money to arrive. The operation was simple. The Bull would load a semi-truck full of drugs and once it was full to capacity, then a call would be made to Benny, who had loaded a semi of his own with money, telling him a time. That meant both trucks were to leave simultaneously. The whole deal went down and they never even had to see each other. Thirty minutes from the time of the phone call, both sides should have their delivery. That was the way it had been working for the last ten years, except for that night.

The little bald Italian man was on his second cigarette in five minutes as he paced back and forth.

"What the fuck is taking so long?" The Bull asked his right hand man, Tony, who then paused to light another cigarette before finishing what he was saying. "It's twenty minutes late."

"It might be caught in traffic," Tony replied.

"What fucking traffic? It's Sunday night. You know what it is, it's those lazy ass niggers. They probably weren't even ready," said The Bull.

Tony knew it was no use to trying to make his boss feel better once The Bull got mad. All he seen was red, which usually ended up being somebody's blood.

"Look, Boss, here it goes right here," Tony said, pointing up the road.

"Good, let's unload the money and get the fuck out of here," replied The Bull. "I gotta funny feeling tonight, make sure security is tight," The Bull continued.

"Gotcha, Boss," Tony replied before walking off to make sure the men were on their jobs.

Thirty minutes away, Benny was just ending his complaining to Silk about how late the delivery was when he saw the semi was pulling in the warehouse. "Make sure security is in place. Let's get this shit unloaded. I got shit to do," Benny said, adjusting his five hundred dollar tie that went perfectly with his five thousand dollar blue Armani suit, which covered his frame to perfection as he made his way toward the semi-truck.

The Bull flicked his cigarette as he walked close to his semi that had parked, and just when he reached the back of the truck, he heard a sound that proved his intuition to be right. Footsteps were coming from inside the trailer. The Bull's men stopped immediately as they heard the footsteps, waiting for The Bull's next command, which was being given with hand gestures that made his men fall into attack position. Six men with machine guns aimed at the back of the trailer while one man crept up, grabbing the door latch and opening it as slowly as possible trying to surprise who was inside.

"Benny, somebody is in there," Silk said, drawing his gun with one hand and holding his boss' back with the other hand, stopping him from getting any closer. With only a whistle from Silk, in seconds, the truck was surrounded.

"Open it up," he yelled, and then one of the men quickly grabbed the handle and pulled the door open, only to find himself looking in the eyes of a natural born killer.

The machine gun fire filled the cool loading dock as The Bull's men let off every round they had into their target, making sure there was no coming back for the predator that now lay dead in the back of the empty trailer.

* * * * *

Looking into the eyes of the killer seemed to freeze every bone in the man's body. His first thought was to run, but the only thing running was the blood from the three massive gashes that left his face wide open. "It's a lion," one of the surrounding men yelled, watching the eight hundred pound beast jump from the back of the truck, giving out a roar that was so loud that the men all froze except for Benny, who took off running to his Benz. The lion gave chase, so quick, the men never got a shot off. Benny had about twenty more steps to the car before he noticed he was being chased by the beast. He cut those twenty steps into ten as the lion got closer. Benny reached out and grabbed the passenger door handle, and almost broke it off pulling it open and diving in, pulling the door closed behind him. The thought that he was safe lasted no longer than the door closing. The lion never stopped running and came smashing into the door and the window, splashing glass across Benny's back. The lion was too big to fit through the window, but the razor sharp paws swiped Benny's leg before he had a chance to pull it out of the way.

"Shoot it, shoot it!" Benny yelled, but the men knew the machine fire would rip through the lion and the Benz. They had to wait for the right moment. The massive lion pulled back out of the window, leaped on the roof of the car, and stood facing the approaching men like he had won the battle. By the loud roar he let out, he was ready for some more, but he never got a chance as Silk gave the command.

"Aim high!" was all you heard as the bullets ripped through the lion. Benny covered up, praying he didn't get shot. Then, there was a great silence and a big boom on the roof over his head. Looking up at the windshield, he could see the paw of the lion dangling while rivers of blood streamed down. Benny opened the driver's door and slid out onto the ground while looking at his leg that was bleeding heavily. His phone in his pocket began ringing. He already knew who it was.

"Yeah," Benny said, answering the phone, still out of breath.

"What the fuck is going on, Benny?" But, The Bull never gave Benny a chance to answer before he continued. "We need to have a talk now. Stay there. I'll be there in ten minutes." Benny just looked at his phone as the call ended.

In what only seemed like five minutes, The Bull's caravan pulled into the warehouse. The Bull could barely let the car he was in stop before he was out of the car with Tony trailing behind him, heading toward Benny. Benny was sitting on a crate with Silk standing next to him. The Bull couldn't help but notice the dead lion on top of Benny's car just like the one his men had killed on the docks. Bull's first thought when his men killed the other lion at the docks was Benny had double crossed him, but seeing the dead lion and Benny's leg bleeding, he knew they had both been fucked.

Silk helped Benny to his feet as The Bull approached.

"Where is my shit?" Benny demanded.

"You got a lot of nerve coming down here without my shit or my money," Benny said. Then, Benny reached and pulled his .45 from his waist that set off a chain reaction of guns being pointed. Silk and Tony were staring down the barrels of each other's guns. The twelve soldiers Bull brought with him were aiming at Benny's twenty men that were aiming at them.

"Just wait a minute, everybody!" The Bull pleaded before continuing. "There was a lion in my truck, also, my friend." Benny couldn't believe what he heard, but he knew there was no way The Bull would've gone down there and put himself in danger like that. "Now if everybody puts their guns down, we can get to the bottom of this," The Bull said, causing Benny to lower his gun and the chain reaction happened all over again, except the guns were now lowered.

"Now, my friend, you need to think carefully about this situation," The Bull said, pausing to light a cigarette, giving Benny one, and turning their back to everybody and walking away out of ear's reach. The Bull continued "Somebody don't like both of us, 'cause this was more than a robbery, it was a message. Whomever could've easily killed the drivers and took the trucks, but it was more to it than that." Before Benny even said anything, he knew that the message was clear as day.

"The King of the jungle," Benny said, not realizing that

he was thinking out loud.

"King of the jungle?" The Bull repeated after Benny, trying to understand.

"Yeah, the message is simple. King has our shit and he is letting us know he's the King of the jungle," Benny said.

"King? I thought he was dead," Benny replied.

"Yeah, that's what they say, but I know better. He is even more dangerous now, 'cause he's like a ghost and he plans to hunt us, as you can see," Benny said.

"Well, if he is behind this, he can't be doing this alone. He would have needed help," The Bull responded.

"He's not, it's his sons and his daughter," Benny replied.

"And, what do you know about them?"

"Shit, the boys, they only sixteen," Benny said.

"Sixteen!" The Bull said, cutting Benny off.

"You standing here telling me that two sixteen year olds and a bitch high-jacked us for two hundred and fifty million dollars, two tons of cocaine, a ton of heroin, and enough guns to supply a country?" Benny didn't answer. "I can't believe this shit" The Bull ranted. "Where are these boys and the bitch?"

"I can handle it," Benny said. "I already got somebody that can get inside as we speak."

"Good, get our shit back or I will." Benny knew what that meant. After The Bull killed the twins and their sister, he would try to kill him.

"I said I can handle it," Benny replied.

* * * * *

Twon and Tish had not stopped talking yet about how easy it was to hit the lick as Twon turned his semi down Harmony Lane with Qwon right behind.

"Them mu'fuckas probably mad as hell right now," Twon said to his sister.

"Mad ain't even the word, we played they ass," Tish responded, laughing out loud as she thought of the plan again in her head.

The plan was simple. The only time to have a chance at the trucks would be in transport, but most of the drive was on the highway. That made it hard until they saw the photos Uncle Red had taken of the trucks at the weight stations, getting special treatment from the state troopers who were definitely on the payroll and never even weighed the trucks. The second mistake they made was renting the trucks from a well-known trucking company, whose trucks were all the same color. Uncle Red took care of getting the trucks, and somehow managed to get two lions in two days. He said their father couldn't help but to throw them in there. The only hard part was taking over the weigh station, which Goldie and some of his squad handled with pleasure.

The officers never had a chance. They were kidnapped at their homes right before their shift started and replaced by Goldie's white guy Andy, who would do anything to get some more of The Beast to stop the nightmares from coming. Then, Trouble got his Uncle Bud, who they gave five hundred dollars and he never asked any questions. They were told what to do and they did it well.

The whole time the drivers thought they were getting their urine tested, Andy and Bud were watching out the window as the twins and Tish changed the license plates and switched the trucks. The drivers never even knew the difference. Even their coffee was still steaming in the truck's cup holder. Tish came out of her deep thought as Twon pulled the big truck in the warehouse where the King and Red were waiting patiently, standing to the side with golden grins on their faces. The garage door closed as the twins and Tish climbed out of the cabs of the trucks. Tish ran around the truck quickly, giving her uncle and dad hugs. The twins approached and Qwon put his arms out, gesturing for his uncle to give him a hug.

"Boy, if you come over here I'm gonna shoot you, Qwon," Red said, laughing at his nephew.

"Y'all cool?" King asked, walking over to the boys, rubbing them on top of their heads.

"Yeah, we cool, Pops," Twon answered for the both of them.

"Good, now let's get these trucks open," King said, walking with the boys to the back of the truck Twon was driving. The twins and Tish knew there was some drugs, but not as much as they saw when Twon pulled the door open. The pallets were full of kilo after kilo.

"Oh Shit!" Qwon said, looking at the drugs. But, that

wasn't all there was. There were crates of at least forty to fifty of them.

"What's the crates?" Twon asked as Uncle Red jumped up on the back of the truck with a crowbar, jamming it into the side of one the huge boxes. He popped the nails out until the front of the crate fell off and out poured AK-47s, M-16s, AR15s, 9s, 45s, and at least a one hundred other guns.

"Let me get this, Pops," Qwon said, grabbing an AK-47.

"Y'all can have whatever y'all want," King said, laughing at how much his sons were like him. King walked over to the next truck, opening it himself. He already knew what was in that one, two hundred and fifty black bags containing a million dollars apiece.

"Twon, come grab y'all a couple of these bags for each of y'all, and grab one for your other two people," King said. Twon quickly ran over to help his dad, jumping up in the truck and throwing eight bags out. King was so proud of his twins and daughter; he wanted to give them the world he thought to himself while he helped his son down out of the truck. He turned his attention to Tish, who was now hanging on his arm, laying her head on his shoulder. It only lasted a second, because Uncle Red and Qwon was at it again.

"That's a vest, Unk," Qwon said to his Uncle Red while watching him pull it out of the second crate.

"What it look like, boy?" Red asked, holding it up.

"Put it on, let's see if it work," Qwon said.

"Boy, if I have to get out of this truck I'm gonna fuck

you up," Red replied, walking toward the end of the truck where Qwon stood. Qwon wasted no time jumping down and walking toward his dad.

"Boy, leave your uncle alone," King said to Qwon, who kept looking over his shoulder for his uncle.

"Unk crazy. I just wanted to see if the vest worked," Qwon said, laughing.

"You crazy," Tish said, joining in her brother's laughter.

"Okay, y'all listen for a minute," King said, pausing as the kids paid attention to what he was about to say. "Y'all did good, but this is only the beginning stages of what is to come. In another week or two, without those drugs, the other two projects are gonna go down, and that's when y'all pick them up and put them on y'all team, and let them eat off y'all plate. In the meantime, I want y'all to take an extra two million off the truck and I want y'all to give back to the hood. I mean, help everybody you can. It's very important, just trust me, Qwon," King said, seeing his son about to ask a question. Then, he continued. "From now on, it's gonna be a target on y'all head from the police, the Feds, the Italians, and Benny's men. That means it's time to elevate y'all game. We're almost at the finish line, a'ight?" Their heads nodding up and down was good enough for King. "Yall be careful," was his last words before throwing a few fake jabs at the twins, then kissing Tish on the head. King walked away thinking to himself, *It won't be long now and they'll all be together again.*

* * * * *

Agent Fellows couldn't believe what he heard as he paced back and forth in Benny's penthouse. "So, you telling me we've lost everything?"

"That's exactly what I'm telling you," Benny said, taking a swig from his glass of Hennessey, and then sitting it back down on his desk. "And, not only that, my sources tell me that it's a new drug being sold out of the Jones that's got white people going crazy," Benny said. "That mu'fucka King, I should've killed him myself that night," Agent Fellows snapped while pouring a drink. "I thought you ran the Jones?" Agent Fellows said while sipping from his glass.

"I did, but the twins and their sister done took over. They done pushed the heroine and the cocaine out of the Jones," Benny replied.

"This just gets better and better," Fellows said, finishing his drink and pouring another one. "Well, how much shit do we got left?" Fellows asked.

"About a week's worth," Benny replied. "How about The Bull, he won't front us none until we get the shit back?" Fellows asked.

"Hell naw, he got The Cartel all over his back already," Benny replied.

"Fuck, that means we're gonna have to apply some pressure and get our shit back. We're not only gonna lose everything in the hood, we're gonna be dead men walking as well," Fellows said, slamming his second glass down before continuing.

"Do what you gotta do, Benny. I got some phone calls to make and see if we can't turn the heat up down there on the twins and their sister," he finished while making his way toward the door.

"I thought you had agents on the twins?" Benny asked while making Agent Fellows stop in his tracks to answer him.

"I did. We still ain't found them yet," Agent Fellows continued out the penthouse door.

Benny picked up his phone and started dialing, holding the receiver to his ear until a voice answered on the other end. Benny never gave the person a chance to speak. He said, "Handle that," and hung the phone up, staring at it while thinking, *I knew having somebody on the inside would pay off, now it is only a matter of time.*

* * * * *

Tuesday would be a day the hood would never forget. Four eighteen-wheelers pulled up in front of the Jones, blocking all traffic completely. The people that were outside couldn't help but to stop and stare, even people in the project windows were trying to see what the hell was going on. The twins, Tish, Trouble, and Goldie were walking across the courtyard toward the trucks, which were parked, and took the positions at the back of the truck door with the drivers waiting on the command to open them up.

"Let's do it!" Qwon yelled to the drivers, who wasted no time opening the truck doors.

The onlookers couldn't believe what they were seeing. Food, clothes, shoes, coats, electronics, toys. You name it, it was in those trucks, and they were being passed out to the hood. People came from one end of the hood to the other, and that was a least ten blocks in every direction with the three projects right in the middle. The twins and Tish were thanked by so many people they were almost overwhelmed. Trouble and Goldie were regular old Santa Clauses. Trouble even had his Santa hat on. Qwon was really touched by a little, old, white haired lady who had to at least be in her eighties.

She stood in front of the twins and Tish, and said, "I knew the King and Queen hadn't forgotten their people." A tear ran down her wrinkled face as she paused for a second, and then continued. "This is your kingdom, young princes and princess, and we are your people—save us, please." Then, she turned around and disappeared into the crowd.

Qwon couldn't help but see why this was so important to his father. All those black people, whether light skin, dark skin, male or female, young or old, were missing love, hope, and unity. At that moment, they were getting all three. Qwon's train of thought was broken by a tug at the bottom of his coat. Qwon looked down to and to his surprise, it was a little black girl with four little pig tails with her brand new pink coat on. Qwon kneeled down, and the little girl gave him a hug and said, "Thank you, Prince."

Within seconds, the twins and Tish were mobbed by little kids hugging them and thanking them. Then, the chant of, "Royalty, royalty," took over the crowd of people. It was so loud, you could probably hear them on the other side of the city. By the time the media arrived, there was no way they could even get close to the projects. The best they could do was get area shots of the five blocks of black people that surrounded the projects.

King watched the news, knowing he had made the right decisions with his kids. He could have easily spoiled them while he was locked up, but he and Queen had a plan, and up to that point, it was going right on schedule. He couldn't do anything but grin as he filled up two champagne glasses.

Benny almost went crazy seeing what was going on down in the hood. "Them mu'fuckas down there giving my money away to those people!" he yelled to Silk right before he kicked the TV over.

* * * * *

Yes, it was a bright day in the hood. Really, the only time black people come together was at a funeral, but it was not a funeral; it was actually the birth of a nation. To lead people that had been lost and blinded by the drugs and poverty would be a heavy burden, but by the conversation that was taking place at the house on the lake, they had every intention of stepping up and carrying it.

"I can't believe that shit," Trouble said, pausing like he was getting his thoughts together before continuing. "I just didn't know so many people are hurting like that."

"Shit, nigga, I been selling rocks and blow to most them people for years, not even knowing the damage I was doing," Goldie added, taking a pull off his Newport.

"I know I didn't grow up there, but that's my home," Tish said.

"No doubt, Sis," Twon said, putting his arm around her shoulder.

"That's home for all of us," Qwon said, standing up and continuing.

"Our Granny lived there, our Granddaddy, our uncles lived there, and our Momma and Daddy lived there. That's most definitely home."

"You right, Bro," Tish said, jumping in on what her brother was saying. "Mu'fuckas should be worried about the pussy ass police, the D.A.s, and the judges locking us up and throwing away the key like they really trying to stop drugs in the hood. All they doing is containing it. Shit, if they stopped it, they wouldn't have a job."

"Half the niggas don't know shit but selling drugs in that hood," Trouble said.

"That's a'right, it won't be long now and won't be anything else to sell but The Beast. The white mu'fuckas gonna bow to the family one way or another," Qwon said, popping the cork out of his Remy VSOP bottle and taking a big gulp. "Family."

"Family."

"Family."

"Family."

"Family," they all said one after another. They knew in their hearts that it was truly their destiny.

* * * * *

The next day was the beginning of a new day in the hood. People walked around with smiles on their faces, waving at the twins and Trouble as they rode through in Qwon's Chevy. It seemed like the day was starting off good until about five or six unmarked squad cars boxed them in at the intersection. Within what seemed like seconds, the twins and Trouble were in the back of squad cars while the police searched the Chevy and turned up with nothing. It still didn't stop them from taking the car and them to the station with no explanation. No sooner than the twins got pulled over, a squad member put the call into Goldie, who wasted no time calling Tish.

"Hello," Tish said.

"Yeah, this is Goldie. They got the twins and Trouble."

"Who got them?" Tish asked.

"The police," replied Goldie.

"For what?" Tish asked.

"Shorty didn't say. He said they got swarmed on by the Dicks, thrown in police cars, and taken to the station," Goldie replied.

"Aight, let me make some calls, family," Tish said.

"Family," Goldie replied, hanging up the phone.

Tish was dressed and out the door fast. She sent Juicy on her way and told her she'd call her later. She had to see what was going with her family. The Benz shot down the highway as she pulled out her cell phone, hitting number one on speed dial. The phone rang until a black lady answered on the other end.

"Mr. Clayton's office. How may I help you?" the lady asked.

"This Latisha Scott," that's all Tish got to say before the secretary cut her off.

"One second, Ms. Scott, let me put you right through," the secretary said as the phone went dead for a second, and then Mr. Clayton's voice filled the silence.

"Tish, you there?" the man asked with his deep voice.

"Yeah, they got the twins and Trouble."

"Alright. I'll meet you at the police station," he said. The line went dead.

Mr. Clayton knew the call was gonna come soon. Since he was King's lawyer, he had to be prepared for anything. As he grabbed his suitcase, he still remembered the night King shot that cop. King had told him to hurry up and get there, and hung the phone up. By the time he got there, King was in the back of a police car smiling. Even the trial was crazy. The Feds got a fake warrant signed by a crooked judge, and with that they convicted King of first degree murder of a law enforcement officer, sentencing King to natural life. King never frowned as the judge sentenced him. He just grinned like he had a secret joke or something.

Mr. Clayton knew what the joke was. At first, he thought he may be dead until one day the doorbell rang at six in the morning. When he opened the door, there was nothing there but a black bag with a million dollars in it, and a manila folder with pictures and names of the twins, Tish, Johnny Biggs aka Goldie, and Tyree Martin aka Trouble. He knew it was time to get his game face on. He hadn't had any big clients since King, but there he was, Dominique Clayton, the best black attorney around, back in action.

"Patrice," he said, walking through his office on his way out the door. "We ain't taking any more clients right now. I think we about to be real busy," he said, closing the door behind him.

* * * * *

Uncle Red had told Tish if anybody got arrested, call Mr. Clayton and he'd handle everything. All she worried about was why they were there in the first place, but she was sure about to find out as she lit her Newport to calm her nerves while waiting in the parking lot for the lawyer to arrive. On the inside, the interrogations were already underway.

"Trouble, Trouble, Trouble," the two hundred and sixty pound, white, bald headed officer said as he walked around the chair where Trouble was sitting in the interrogation room. The interrogation room was different than your normal one. It had a two-way mirror, no window and no camera, just a table and a chair. "There's some very important questions I'm gonna ask you, and you're gonna tell me the truth and nothing but the truth," the officer said, rolling his sleeves up in a tactic to intimidate Trouble. It was not working as Trouble sat back in his chair and crossed his arms.

All he said was, "Fuck you and your questions."

The twins were in a similar room to the one Trouble was in, only their room had one side with a window and on the other side of the window was Agent Fellows, watching the twins make fools out of those officers. The officers still didn't know who Twon and Qwon was.

"What's your fucking name?" the red headed officer from the drug task force demanded while pointing at Qwon. His partner with the dark hair jumped up from the table he was sitting at across from the twins and slammed his hand down on the table, showing his frustration.

"Enough fucking games. Fuck your names, what the fuck is this shit y'all selling out the projects?" the officer asked. The officer's emotions were getting the best of him, considering his son and his wife were victims of The Beast and were probably out trying to score right now.

"You think you scare a nigga 'cause your face all red and you hitting tables? Fuck you and you and, how about that," Qwon said.

Both the twins started laughing, and the dark haired officer had to be held back by his partner as tear began to run down his face. "I'll kill you two little mu'fuckas right now!" he said, reaching for his gun, but his partner held his arms as the door flew open and agent Fellows walked in.

"That's enough, officers, go get some air," Agent Fellows said, pointing for the two officers to leave.

"You heard him, go get some air, cry baby," Qwon taunted the officer on their way out the door, slamming it behind them.

Fellows walked around the table, looking at the twins and wondering if they recognized him, but they had their game faces on so it was hard to tell at the moment. He wasted no more time, knowing soon somebody else would be watching through the window. "I'm not here to ask any questions, actually I'm here to give y'all a chance, and one chance only. First, I want both the trucks y'all high-jacked the other night with everything that was in them fully intact. Second, I want that shit your fathers got y'all selling off the streets and y'all disappear!" The twins never flinched a bit at what Fellows was saying. He continued. "If these, shall we say, chances aren't taken, I will do everything in my power to destroy y'all and your family once and for all!" At that moment was when the Twon's mind remembered who the agent was that was talking to them.

"Bro, that's the dude that was at our house with Benny that night Pop's went to jail," Twon said.

"Wow, that must mean you're the smart one," Agent Fellows said, really not caring if they knew who he was or not. He just wanted his product back, them dead and King. Next time he'd do it himself to make sure it was done.

"Well, first I want you to kiss my ass, and second, I want you to kiss his ass!" Qwon said, and then the twins started laughing.

"Yall think this is a game!" Fellows said, raising his voice, hating to be made a fool of. "Your father has the world fooled, but not me. I'm gonna hunt him down and kill him while y'all watch!"

"Like when we watched him shoot your buddy's face off that night?" Qwon said. Before Fellows could answer, the door flew open and in walked the captain followed by Mr. Clayton, who wasted no time making his presence felt.

"This interview is over! My clients have nothing to say. They are underage and we will be filing a civil suit for false arrest and harassment," Mr. Clayton said pausing, helping the twins up out of there seat. "I see you haven't given up yet, Agent Fellows!" Then, the lawyer laughed as he walked his clients out with the captain right behind him. "Now, where is Mr. Martin?" Before the captain could answer, the loud booming sound coming from the other interrogation room caught their attention.

All the captain could think to himself was, *Please, don't let the officer be in there applying a little police justice, especially not with this lawyer here.* He paused for a second, and then turned the door knob and opened it, only to see the officer and Trouble wrestling up against the wall.

"I'm gonna kill you, you black mu'fucka!" the officer said, not noticing the door had opened.

"Get your hands off my client!" Those words snapped the officer back to reality and he let go. The captain could see blood coming from Trouble's mouth, but when the officer turned around, you could clearly see that Trouble had got the best of the fight. The officer's right eye was closed shut and was swollen like he had a golf ball under his eye lid.

"What is going on here?" Mr. Clayton demanded.

"This pussy ass officer snaked me, so I defended myself!" Trouble said, spitting blood out on the floor. The officer didn't say anything, he knew he had underestimated the fat boy and paid the price.

"Let's go, Mr. Martin!" Mr. Clayton said, holding the door open for his client to walk by. "I got a busy day ahead of me filing complaints and lawsuits!" Mr. Clayton said, walking off with his clients, leaving the captain and the officer speech-less.

"Damn, you good." Twon said to Mr. Clayton.

"You ain't seen nothing yet," he replied, opening the front door of the police station where a crowd of people and reporters made it almost impossible to walk through. as the lawyer pushed his clients toward the black Cadillac limo he had waiting on them. Once by the limo, Mr. Clayton stopped to talk to the media as questions flew one after another.

"Mr. Clayton, what were your clients charged with?" a reporter asked.

"Absolutely nothing. This was an attempt to intimidate my clients. My clients and I have great remorse for the twelve dead officers that were slain, but their father was slain as well. As you can see, one of my clients has been struck in the mouth and if I wouldn't have got here in time, there is no telling what else would have happened. These officers are out of control, and I assure you that we will be filing lawsuits by the end of the day!" Mr. Clayton said, and then opened the door of the limo so his clients and him could get in. Once the door closed, the limo pulled off from the curb.

"Where all them people come from?" Qwon asked.

"I called them. It's a tactic to keep the police off of you and when we file these million dollar lawsuits, they really gonna back up!" The lawyer said in an arrogant voice.

"How about my car?"

"Oh, it's been released and towed to the projects for you."

"Damn, Mr. Clayton, you be on it," Twon said.

"Yeah, I do, don't I?" he responded, making them laugh as the limo pulled up at the projects. "If y'all need me, call me. Twenty-four hours a day, a'ight?"

"Aight," Qwon said, answering for them, really getting a kick out of how cool their lawyer was.

People were standing around as Trouble and the twins got out the limo. Tish was the first one they saw as she ran up hugged them. The onlookers cheered for them like they were heroes as they made their way in the building Goldie was in waiting on them. Goldie was rolling a blunt when they came in the apartment, but got up to show them some love.

"Y'all good?"

"Hell yeah, they wasn't on shit. They were trying to scare us, that's all," Twon said, flicking the lighter to light the already rolled blunt Goldie gave him. "They gonna turn the heat up around here, but we ready!" Goldie said, licking the backwood blunt full of hydro closed.

"What happened to you?" Goldie asked, looking at Trouble.

Before he could answer, Qwon did. "He let the police beat his ass."

"You crazy as hell, you seen his eye, nigga," Trouble said.

"His eye, he hit the police in the eye?" Goldie asked, almost choking on the blunt.

"Hell yeah, the police eye was like dude in *Friday*," Qwon said, causing them all to laugh as they engaged in a smoke session.

* * * * *

It was Friday morning and in the projects, you would've thought somebody had died by the amount of people that were outside. Slim had woke Goldie up to come see the scene for himself. Once Goldie got out the bed and looked out the window, he couldn't help but smile because he knew exactly what was happening out there in the streets. The drought had just hit hard. Dope fiends were walking around clueless to what was really going on and the heroin addicts knew exactly what was going on , they couldn't get their fix, meaning they were surely gonna get sick in a way that was unexplainable. Some say they would rather die, some say it was the only reason they got high. Whatever the case was, they were sure about to find out.

"Qwon, y'all need to get down here and see this shit!" Goldie said into his cell phone.

"Aight, nigga, we on our way, family!"

"Family!" Goldie said, hanging up his cell phone as he stood in the doorway of the building next to Slim, shaking his head as the hundred to two hundred people searched for the drug that has been destroying they life for years. Some longer than others, but whatever the case, it was day one in the rehab program that they had no choice but to sign up for. The day was so unbelievable, Qwon and Goldie was still talking about it as they looked down on the packed crowd at the Red Light later on that night.

"Man, I still can't believe ain't no dope in the hood!" Goldie said, sipping Remy from his glass.

"You could probably sell a rock for a hundred dollars right now," Qwon added, taking a pull from his Newport, turning around to see Tish and Juicy approaching.

"Where y'all going?" Qwon asked.

"We fixing to get up out of here and hit the crib up," Tish answered. Qwon could see why, looking at Juicy in her tight ass Apple Bottom jeans that look like her ass and thighs were just meant for them. The low cut waist showing her pink G-string off from the front to the back made Qwon sure wanna find out why they called her Juicy.

"Damn, it's still an hour till the club let out," he said.

Tish didn't reply, she slapped Juicy across her ass and waved bye to her brother and Goldie, who couldn't do nothing but shake their heads and laugh.

"Fuck it, nigga, let's get in here with Twon and Trouble, they been in V.I.P all night," Goldie said, tapping Qwon on the arm before they walked off to see what was going down in V.I.P.

For the next hour, they kicked it and made their choices for the after party. When the club let out, it was the usual scene, the stretch Hummer was outside loading up the twelve females for the after party. The lemon lime Chevys pulled off from the curb with the Hummer right behind them. The people from the club were everywhere like normal when the club let out, niggas with tight whips showing off like it was a car show.

Twon and Trouble were in the first Chevy that pulled up to the stop light. Qwon and Goldie were right on their bumper in the other Chevy, arguing about who had the baddest bitch for the night, which they both knew Tish had. When the light turned green, a black SUV sped across the intersection, pulling right in front of Twon's Chevy, blocking him in. They never even saw the other two SUVs next to them in the turning lane. The passenger windows of the SUVs went down and the machine gun fire filled the night air and the Chevys, never giving the twins a chance to get to their stash spots.

* * * * *

Tish laid in her yellow panties and bra, sitting with her legs spread apart watching Juicy strip down to nothing but those pink G-string panties, showing off her creamy peanut butter complexion as she climbed on the bed in between Tish's thighs. She slowly tasted them from her knees until she pulled Tish's panties to the side, tasting her sweet center. Tish grabbed the back of Juicy's head, grinding her waist as that fat pussy leaked all over. Tish couldn't hold it in any longer, she screamed out Juicy's name as her body began to shake, letting her juices explode all over Juicy's face. "Ooh, get all that shit, Juicy!" Tish said, ready to return the pleasure she'd just received. Tish and Juicy laid next to each other kissing softly on the lips while Tish played in between Juicy's legs, and then began kissing her way down her stomach. Right when she got to Juicy's soaking wet pussy ,all the power in the house went out.

* * * * *

The scene outside the Red Light was chaos. The screams

were horrific and unforgettable. The air was full of gun smoke from the almost three hundred rounds of ammunition that riddled the Chevys' paint jobs. When the SUVs pulled off after letting off the last rounds, it seemed as if everything went in slow motion. Goldie's right hand man, Slim, was in the parking lot trying to get out when the gunfire let off. He found himself running toward the Chevys that showed no movement coming from them. The onlookers that weren't running couldn't believe what they had just seen; some cried, some were still in shock. Slim was about ten to fifteen feet away when the bullet riddled driver's door of Qwon's car started creeping open. Slim stopped dead in his tracks by the fear of what he'd see.

* * * * *

"What happened to all the power?" Juicy asked, watching Tish get up and put on her little pajama shorts and shirt.

She didn't respond as she reached under the bed and came back up and cocking the M-16 she held in her hand while reaching down again and grabbing a black shoulder bag and throwing it over her shoulder. She paused for a second and reached under the pillow, pulling out her pink Colt .45. "Here, take this!" Tish said, passing the .45 to Juicy, who was standing up. "All you gotta do is aim and squeeze. It's already ready to go!" Tish continued telling Juicy while walking out the bedroom door.

"What's going on, Tish?" Juicy asked nervously.

"Stay here, I'll be back!" Tish replied, creeping out the bedroom door and closing it behind her.

* * * * *

Slim's body froze, surely looking at death. "Qwon, it's me!" Slim said, pausing. "Qwon, is you alright?" Qwon didn't respond as he almost fell out the Chevy, obviously disoriented and maybe even in shock, not knowing how he was still alive and walking. He pointed his two Desert Eagle's in Slim's direction. "They gone, nigga!" Slim said, but Qwon turned toward his brother's Chevy and ran toward it as fast as he could.

"Twon, Twon!" As he got closer, he saw the passenger door of Twon's Chevy open, and out came Twon holding his two Eagles at his side with Trouble getting out shaking his head, not believing they were still alive. "What the fuck, y'all good?" Qwon said, looking his brother over.

"Yeah, we good. Y'all good?" Twon said, now seeing Goldie in the street with Slim. The onlookers couldn't believe what they saw, both Chevy bodies ate up by bullets, but all the windows were intact and nobody was bleeding or dead.

"Nobody told us these mu'fuckas was bulletproof!" Qwon said, still trying to catch his breath. Uncle Red threw that feature on the Chevys. They were equipped with bulletproof glass and armor proofing under the paint jobs. That was his little surprise he'd hoped they'd never need, but it was always better safe than dead.

"Where's Tish?" Twon asked his brother, looking concerned.

"She at the house!" Qwon replied, realizing her life could be in danger as well.

"We gotta warn her!" Twon said, already on the phone calling as Slim pulled up in his Cadillac truck. "There's no answer!" Twon said as they all jumped in the truck and peeled off on their way to the house on the lake.

* * * * *

Tish made her way slowly down the hallway toward the living room, looking toward the windows that had six red laser beams flashing through. Tish ducked down low and released the powerful M-16 toward the direction the beams were coming from. The windows instantly were blown out by the bullet's that hit two of her targets. The return fire ripped back, slamming bullets into the walls and tearing the living room apart. Tish stayed low as she ran toward the stairs, diving to avoid the bullets that smashed into the wall above her head. She had no time to rest, the front door and the garage door seemed to fly off the hinges and what had looked to be six assassins quickly turned to twelve. *Ain't this some bullshit?* she thought as she made her dash up the stairs with machine gunfire close on her heels. "Fuck this, that's enough of this running shit!" she whispered to herself, thinking out loud.

The assassins stopped shooting, moving into position to

go up the stairs, but the first man that stepped on the stairs seemed to be ripped in half by Tish's M-16. She was laying on her stomach at the top of the stairs, using the darkness to her advantage. The assassins hit the floor quickly, amazed at her accuracy, even in the dark. They waited for about thirty seconds, and then they heard a door from upstairs open and close. They quickly gathered themselves, shooting off a couple rounds up the stairs just in case Tish was fooling them. They moved quickly up the stairs, but cautiously, letting the red beams scan everything. Five of them took position outside the first bedroom while the other four attempted to walk down the hallway toward the other bedroom before Tish sent bullets slicing through the walls. They tried to get out the way, but it was no hope as she let off fifty rounds in about five seconds, filling the four men with slugs. The other five men returned fire, but it was way too late. All they heard was Tish laughing as she loaded another clip, ready for her next kill. The assassins knew they had to get into that room and kill that bitch. Too bad they didn't know the bedrooms were connected, but they quickly found out as the other bedroom opened and Tish opened fire again, that time hitting two of her targets while the other three made a retreat down the stairs. They got to the bottom of the stairs and knew they had made their last step. It was like seeing doubles.

"Where the fuck y'all going!" Qwon asked as he and Twon stood there with their Desert Eagles aimed, squeezing their triggers with hatred in every squeeze until all four guns were empty and the three assassins' bodies crumbled to the floor in front of them, lying next to the body Tish had left behind. They looked up and there was Tish coming down the stairs. The lights popped on, meaning Goldie and Trouble had found the fuse box. Tish was happy as hell to see her brothers standing there.

"Damn, I think I broke a nail!" she said, looking at her hand as she walked by the twins, who looked at her like she was crazy as they watched her walk toward her bedroom.

"Damn, it look like a war done went on in this mu'fucka!" Trouble said as he, Goldie, and Slim came in through the front door that was now lying on the floor.

Tish opened the bedroom door. "Juicy!" she said as she only got a foot in the room before she felt cold steel pressed against her head. Tish dropped her gun as her assassin walked her back out in the hallway for everyone to see.

"What the fuck!" Qwon said, making everybody's attention turn toward Tish standing in the hallway with a gun on her head and Juicy was holding it. "Juicy, what the fuck you on? Put that gun down," Twon said calmly, trying not to make matters worse.

"Shut the fuck up!" Juicy replied. "I'm here to do a job, I'm gonna get it done!" Juicy squeezed the trigger, sending the hammer popping forward. Everyone's heart skipped a beat as they were helpless for Tish, but the clapping sound was a sound they'd never forget, especially since Tish was smiling and the clapping sound was her hands coming together. She then turned around and faced Juicy, whose face looked like she'd seen a ghost.

"Wow, you should get an award for acting like a killa, bitch!" Tish said. Juicy pulled the trigger two more times, but she knew like everybody else in the house that the gun was empty. Her thoughts disappeared into darkness as Tish hit her with a quick left to her chin and an overhand right to the jaw, knocking her out cold.

* * * * *

The call at three a.m. to Mr. Clayton's house phone almost made him jump out the bed. "Hello!" he answered as he woke up.

"Mr. Clayton!" Tish said through the phone. Hearing her voice, Mr. Clayton immediately woke up, knowing something must have happened while he was deep in his dreams.

"Yes, yes!" he said, waiting in anticipation for her response.

"I think you should get down here to our house!"

"Don't say no more, I'm on my way!" Mr. Clayton said, hanging up the phone and throwing his clothes on. Within five minutes, he was on his way to the house on the lake. In the back of his mind, he couldn't help but think shit couldn't be good as his Benz sped down the highway.

* * * * *

Upon arriving close to the area surrounding the house,

Mr. Clayton could clearly see something big had gone down. He had to park almost two blocks away, there was no way he was gonna be able to get through. The streets were covered with reporters, bystanders, police, and ambulances. The flashing lights from the sirens seemed to light the night up as Mr. Clayton made his way through the people, only being stopped by the reporters that recognized him and quickly started throwing questions at him. The officer protecting the yellow tape lifted the it, pointing the lawyer toward his client that he could see sitting on the back of an ambulance wrapped in a blanket. As the paramedics checked her out, Mr. Clayton couldn't help but to overhear a couple of officers talking as he walked by.

"There are at least twelve bodies inside!" He couldn't believe what he was hearing.

At least she wasn't in handcuffs he thought as he approached his client.

"Excuse me!" he said to the paramedics. "Could I have a moment alone with my client?" The paramedics just gave him a nod and walked off. Mr. Clayton climbed in the back of the ambulance and closed the doors behind him, giving them some privacy to discuss what had just happened.

"Twelve bodies!" he said, looking at Tish who was grinning, reminding him of her father.

Red had the news on as King walked in the office at the warehouse. King looked at the screen, seeing his sons' Chevys covered with bullet holes, and a reporter telling what happened. *"Were outside club Red Light where an apparent assassination attempt was made against the Scott Twins, the sons of the deceased Tyler Scott, also known as King, who was recently the victim of an assassination. From what the police have told us, three black SUVs blocked the Chevy Caprices in and opened fire!"* the report said, pausing and pointing at the bullet riddled Chevys before continuing. *"There are no suspects at this time, and strangely enough, no victims, either. The police are reporting that the Chevys were bullet proof, and they are doing their best to locate the twins, but they are nowhere to be found at this time!"*

"Thanks, Deb," the news anchor in the studio said, cutting her off. *"We have breaking news, and we will keep you informed of the shooting at the club as details unfold. Now, we'd like to take you live to the scene of another apparent assassination.*

Bob, you there?"

"Yeah, I hear you good, Rich," the blond haired reporter said.

"Well what's going on down there?"

"Right now, we are getting little information and cooperation from the police. The word going down is eight to ten dead bodies inside this lake home behind me, and there's possibly more. This home belongs to LaTisha Scott, also known as King's daughter, and the sister of the Scott twins, who were the victim of an assassination attempt earlier tonight. At this point, she's the only one that's come

out alive, and is now in the back of an ambulance with the notorious defense attorney, Dominique Clayton."

Red turned the news off, looking at his brother whose face displayed a look that Red knew so well. It was that face that meant bodies were surely about to start turning up, and they usually turned up without their heads.

"How you want to do this, Bro?" Red asked, leaning back in his chair, waiting on an answer.

"These mu'fuckas want a war? We might as well give them what they want. I mean, what kind of people would we be if we didn't help them out?" The King said as he and Red started laughing simultaneously, knowing in both of their cold hearts that the beginning was had come, and even though they started it, they definitely were gonna finish it as well.

* * * * *

Mr. Clayton made quick work of the detectives and the media at the house on the lake. He explained a clear case of self-defense, even though he could hardly believe that the pretty faced female that had just got out his Benz and was walking toward the Marion Jones project buildings had just left twelve bodies behind without even a scratch on her that he could see.

Tish made her way into the first building, giving nods to the squad members that were standing outside the door as she entered. She was then escorted by another squad member to a door that led to the basement. The room at the bottom of the stairs was empty, but she could see a light coming from under the door that was across the dark room she was walking. The door opened up as she reached it, and Tish never stopped her stride, just gave a nod to the squad member that opened the door for her and closed it behind her.

"About time!" Qwon said, walking toward his sister, greeting her with the blunt he and the rest of the Family was smoking on while waiting on her.

"Whatever, nigga!" she said, taking the blunt and hitting it before continuing.

"Where she at?" she asked, blowing the Hydro smoke out.

"Come on," Qwon said, turning around and leading Tish toward another closed door. The closer she got, she could hear what sounded like dog's barking. Qwon opened the door for his sister.

"After you, Sis!" he said, letting her enter first. A grin quickly took over her face as she looked at Twon and Trouble sitting at a table rolling blunts while Goldie stood in the middle of the floor with two chains wrapped around his forearms that were used to hold back two of the biggest red nose pit bulls she'd ever seen. Chained to a pole in the floor, only about eight inches out of the pit bulls' reach, was Juicy begging for her life. Juicy's attention quickly turned for a second to see Tish walking on the room.

"Sit!" Goldie yelled to the dogs that were apparently well trained, because the once crazed pit bulls instantly sat down and didn't make another sound, not even to the approaching Tish who walked over and patted them on the heads.

"Tish, Tish, please!" Juicy started saying before Tish cut her off.

"Shhh," Tish said putting her finger over her lips, letting her know it was time to be quiet. "Juicy, Juicy, Juicy!" Tish said, shaking her head before bending down in front of Juicy. "What a pretty face," she said, stroking her hand across Juicy's face, and then standing back up before continuing. "I must admit, you had me fooled for a while, but if for one minute you'd think I'd die over some pussy, then the only one fooled was you!"

"Tish, please, Benny made me do it. He said he'd kill me if I didn't!"

"Well, I think we should call and give him an update," Tish said, pulling Juicy's phone out her pocket and looking at the screen. "I wonder what number is his, maybe it's the one that's called about fifty times, huh?" Juicy knew she was in a bad situation and chose to cooperate.

"I'll show you, just don't kill me!" Tish showed Juicy the numbers that had called until Juicy said, "That's it right there!" Tish called the number, and then put the phone to Juicy's ear. After two rings, Benny picked up.

"Benny!" That was all Juicy got to say before Tish took the phone from Juicy's ear and put it to hers.

"What the fuck happened?" Benny yelled through the phone. The response he got was one that sent chills down his spine.

"You fucked up!" Tish said, nodding to Goldie. Goldie only said one word.

"Hit!" The word sent the pit bulls into a frenzy. Juicy tried to move, but the pits hit her swiftly. One pit sank his razor sharp teeth into her face, making her scream with pain as the pit's jaw locked and began to shake viciously. The second pit locked on the side of her neck, ripping into her flesh. Benny couldn't believe what he was hearing, and then the phone went dead. Benny couldn't do anything but shake his head as a sick feeling filled the pit of his stomach. He was stuck looking at his phone when Silk spoke. "What happened, Boss?"

"We fucked up!"

Part Five

Blood In

Over the next two weeks, things were quiet after the two assassination attempts, except for the money counters in Marion Jones that seemed to never stop. The family was staying in the Jones, knowing it would take an army to come get them out. The addicts that had been slaves to their drugs for so long were now breaking those chains. Some couldn't believe they were free, others didn't want to be free, but by the smiles on their faces, you could tell they were getting used to it more and more day by day. The only ones in the hood that weren't smiling were Big Block and Blow from the other two projects. Since the drought hit, they'd been hurting for real, but they were hoping all that was about to change as they entered Goldie's apartment in the Jones. Goldie greeted them with handshakes and semi hugs before he spoke.

"Man, I'm happy you could come down and holla at me!" Goldie said, showing them to their seats as he took his seat across from them at his desk that was sitting in the middle of the living room. Big Block and Blow couldn't help but think to themselves that nigga was getting major money. His apartment resembled a boss' office in a billion dollar cooperation.

"Damn, Goldie, y'all niggas eating good down here!" Blow said, looking at the two thousand gallon fish tank on the wall with three little sharks swimming around in it.

"We doing a little something. Let me get y'all a drink!" Goldie said and paused before calling out toward the kitchen.

"Ki Ki, let us get some drinks, sweetie." While they waited on the drinks, Goldie reached in the drawer of his desk, pulling out a box of cigars full of Backwoods that were already rolled full of Kush. He offered them to his two guest, who quickly accepted the offer. By the time the cigars were lit, in walked a short, brown skinned female that was wearing barely nothing.

"Here's y'all drinks," Ki Ki said, turning around and strutting her big, thick, bow legged ass, knowing that she had full attention of the room.

"Thanks, Ki Ki," Goldie said, watching her walk away.

"What's really good, Goldie?" Big Block asked, turning around in his chair watching Ki Ki walk away.

"Life is good, niggas, that's what's up!" Goldie paused, hitting his blunt a couple times before continuing. "It's a new day down here for real. I mean, I know you see it and ain't no reason why y'all can't be a part of this shit. We all grew up together getting money down here." Big Block and Blow just nodded their head in agreement as Goldie continued. "Yeah, we done had our differences over the years, but it's time we come together, niggas!"

"So, what you saying is we combine with y'all?" Blow asked for Big Block and him.

Goldie quickly responded, "That's exactly what I'm saying! If we become one big army with us at the top, of course, I promise you nothing can stop us. The same operation we're running down here, we'll set up in the other two projects. You inform y'all people we merging and from now on we're one big squad, the Goon Squad!" Big Block and Blow shook their heads, still agreeing with Goldie. They couldn't help but think to themselves that the shit sounded real good. Their thoughts were broken by what Goldie said next. "I mean, I ain't trying to brag, but ,niggas, I'm making about two, maybe three million a week!" Their mouths almost hit the floor. "So, what y'all wanna do?"

"I'm in!" Big Block replied.

"Me too!" Blow added.

"Let's do this shit then!" Goldie said, pulling out two stacks of money with fifty thousand dollar bands around each stack, throwing them to Big Block and Blow.

"I think I like this shit already! "Blow said, fanning the money in front of his face before continuing. "I ain't even gonna lie, it's about time we all stood together as one instead of fighting each other over selling shit to our own people. That shit you and the Family pulled down here, cleaning this shit up down here some real ass shit!"

"Hell yeah. I feel the same way. It's a new day down here!" Big Block added, pausing to hit his blunt.

"It's the day of the Goon Squad!"

"I'll toast to that!" Goldie said, standing up and walking around his desk with his glass of Remy as Big Block and Blow stood up with their glasses. "To the birth of the Goon Squad!" Goldie said, holding his glass up to meet theirs.

"Goon Squad!" "Goon Squad!" Big Block and Blow said, toasting with Goldie.

Goldie couldn't help but think to himself there was nothing that could stop them now. Goldie wasted no time reporting the success of the meeting with the other two projects as he stood in the middle of the twins' old apartment. The twins and Tish had remodeled it since they were staying there. Big screen T Vs, new furniture, you name it, they had it. The only thing they didn't change was their mother's bed, which Tish had been sleeping in since they moved in.

"I knew they would get down with the team," Goldie said, having a seat on the black leather couch that sat in front of the sixty-two inch big screen that had *Belly* playing on it.

"That's good!" Tish said, walking into the room with her

blunt in between her fingertips, passing it to Trouble, who was sitting on the edge of the couch. "Now all we gotta do is set the next plan into motion!"

"The next plan should be giving The Bull bitch ass the business!" Qwon said, cutting his sister off. He'd been ready to get The Bull since Uncle Red told him that The Bull had sent that hit squad at them after the club that night.

"Hell yeah, Bro!" Twon added, giving his brother some dap.

"Oh ,we at his ass fa sho!" he finished saying.

"What about Benny?" Trouble asked.

"The word is he in hiding," Goldie said. "But, don't even trip, we got niggas watching for him to pop his head up and when he do, we gone knock it off!" Tish couldn't help but grin as she listened to the ambitions of the Family. The thought of retaliation built moisture in her panties and she quickly had to bring herself back before she reached a climax.

"Oh, we gone get they ass in due time!" Tish said, pausing before continuing. "But, first we got some planning to do, 'cause this shit we about to pull off gone go down in history. We only got to Friday to pull this shit off together, that only gives us four days!"

"Damn, I like the way this shit sound already," Qwon added, grinning from ear to ear.

* * * * *

The cry for unity was long overdue. For years the hood was nothing but a concrete jungle, full of natural born predators, whose instincts to survive turned into cannibals devouring their own kind just to feed their families. They not only had to protect themselves from each other , they had to watch for the hunters dressed in the blue uniforms with their guns and badges, that were quick to snatch fathers away from their young with no remorse for the family that was destroyed. They were taught to hate each other instead of love in order to confuse them and keep them blind to who the real enemy was. With the three projects coming together, a light was shining on the hood and the blind could see. It didn't matter if they were BDs, GDs, 4s, or Moes, it was one family now and the Goon Squad was its name.

It had only been three days since the meeting with Goldie, Big Block, and Blow, and the count was in. They were one hundred and seventy-two soldiers strong and rising by the day. With a small army of men and woman ready and willing to ride or die for the cause, it was time for the families' master plan to go into effect.

* * * * *

Even though The Bull had taken a loss on the deal with Benny, guns and drugs were just a small part of his empire. The Bull had been the number one cappo in the Razzo family for years. He owned the city, his casino was one of the largest in America, and produced seventy-five percent of the city's income. When you made income like that for the city, you became untouchable. The Bull definitely used that power to his advantage. The casino made money on top of money, but his real cash cow was his import/export business he ran from the docks. It was obvious that the drugs and guns came in through there, but his biggest import was the exotic cars that had been stolen in other countries, sticker tagged, and sent to him for resale in the United States. The Bull was estimated to almost be worth a billion dollars and you could tell by the way he smiled as he sat in one of his pizza parlors with Tony discussing how the twins had seemed to disappear off the face of the map since the night outside the club.

"So, there's no news yet?" The Bull asked Tony as he took a pull of his cigarette.

"Nothing yet, Boss. It's like they went into hiding or something!"

"First Benny, now them. That's all these niggers seem to be good at, they tuck their tails and hide in trees like the little monkeys they are," The Bull said, causing him and Tony to start laughing until they were interrupted by the approaching bodyguard who was holding a cell phone in his hand.

"What is it?" Tony asked the bodyguard, who looked like he was scared to answer.

"B...B...Boss!" the bodyguard said, stuttering his words out. "I...I think you should take this call." Tony grabbed the phone out of his hand and put it to his ear.

"What!" Tony snapped, showing his authority in his voice. He closely listened to what was being told to him from the other end of the phone. The Bull sat impatiently staring at Tony trying to read his facial expressions, and by the look on his face it was something most definitely bad. The Bull couldn't take the suspense any longer and demanded to know what was going on.

"What! What! What!" The Bull demanded, slamming his fist down on the table. Tony knew why the bodyguard was stuttering and his facial expression looked as if he'd seen a ghost.

"Boss!" Tony said, pausing as he hung up the phone. "We have a major problem!"

Friday night was one of the casino's biggest days. Tour buses filled the parking lots and people filled the casino, spending their money with the hope of hitting it big. The casino ran like clockwork, never missing a beat.

It was three thirty p.m. when the armored truck pulled up in front of the casino. *Right on time*, the casino boss thought as he watched the heavyset driver and his light skinned partner make their way inside to pick up the casino's money. It was too bad he wasn't the only one watching. The money room was heavily guarded. At any time it was known to have at least fifty million to one hundred million dollars kept back there. It was always at least six armed guards in the room, eight as the armored car drivers were loading the three million dollars the casino wanted to deposit on to their dollies. Everything was going as usual until the casino boss saw a tour bus pull up in front of the casino. What he seen next almost blew his mind. He just picked up the emergency phone and started dialing.

* * * * *

The docks were usually quiet, but it was a shipment day and at least a hundred new cars had come in along with enough guns to fill half a warehouse. The boss down there was happy they were almost done and everything was going smooth, but that ended when he received the call from the casino with a code red, which meant send back –up now!

* * * * *

As the casino boss hung up the phone, he never took his eyes off the security screen watching the thirty armed men exit the bus dressed in all black with black hoods on their heads. Their faces were hidden by the ski masks that covered themfrom their nose down to their chin. In any robbery, they were trained to look for something noticeable they could remember for the police, but that wasn't hard considering the ski mask they wore were airbrushed to look like the mouth of a lion. Entering the casino, the Goon Squad moved in swiftly, shooting in the air to let people know it was not a game. The floor security jumped into action, trying to stop what was happening. Gunfire broke out as the people screamed and hit the floor, trying to dodge bullets that were coming from all directions. Two security guards were almost decapitated by the machine gun fire that hit them. Another one never even got a chance to draw his fire arm before the bullets ripped through his body. The security knew they were outnumbered and out gunned, and the remaining security guards chose to surrender. One of the Squad members stood on a crap table as the rest of the Squad members moved into positions around the casino.

"We're not here to hurt anybody. If you wanna live, I expect your full cooperation and this will be over as soon as possible. I want everybody face down, hands out in front of you, and no talking. You follow these three simple rules, and I assure you that you will be able to go home to your families in one piece."

When he finished talking, he held up a closed fist and his soldiers quickly lined up outside the door that led to the money room, standing patiently and waiting on their next signal. When the casino boss saw that, he knew it was time to go into a defensive procedure they had practiced many times before.

"Let's do it," the red haired security boss yelled.

His men quickly went into action. Four of the security guards grabbed machine guns out of the gun cabinet and made their way into the hallway, taking aim at the door that stood between them and the squad. Once the door shut to the money room it locked from the inside, and just in case someone did make it past the four guards in the hallway, the doors and the walls were made of a material that would take a tank to get through. It just so happened they made it into the money room the other two guards, which was now four since the armored car drivers were caught in the middle, would be waiting. Just for an extra precaution, the casino boss was got his oxygen tank out of the closet, preparing to lock himself in the vault. He knew all they had to do was wait for back up to arrive. Little did he know, back up was needed at another location.

When the phone call came in from the docks for back up at the casino, the boss at the docks quickly assembled twenty out of the thirty of The Bull's soldiers and sent them to the casino. Two guards stood at the gate leading into the docks with M-16s in their hands like they were two military police. Looking down the road, the younger of the two guards spotted an eighteen wheeler approaching.

"I thought we were done with shipments for the day?" the young guard said to the white haired guard.

"Let me double check the list," the older man said, walking toward the little booth to check his clipboard, and then popping back out to tell the younger guard what he had found out .

"We got the shipments done. I'm gonna call up to the warehouse to see if they are expecting something else coming in."

As he dipped back in picking up the phone to call the

boss, the younger guard made his way out into the road, flagging his arm and his rifle in the air so the driver would slow down while his partner checked things out. Only, the truck didn't slow down, it actually sped up and was covering ground very quickly. The younger guard continued waving his arms, thinking to himself, *This mu'fucka has to be crazy driving up that fast.* Little did he, know he was right. Young Blow hit the blunt one more time before passing it to Big Block, who was sitting in the passenger seat of the speeding truck that was only twenty feet away from the front gate with only the young guard standing in their way.

"I think they want us to honk the horn," Blow said, blowing the Hydro smoke out of his nose.

"Fuck it, nigga, help the man out," Block replied as he cocked the AK-47 he had in between his legs.

The young guard knew that the truck had no intentions of stopping, especially since the driver was pulling the air horns on the truck and the truck's speed never slowed down. He did his best to take aim, only getting off two shots before he found himself diving to the side of the road to avoid being hit. The old man wasn't as lucky as the truck roared through the gate and the guard house without even slowing down a bit. The truck went another twenty feet or more and slid to a stop. The rest of the guards that were left behind were hurrying out the warehouses to see, but by the time they got to where the truck was, the back of the truck had come open and thirty Squad members with AKs, hoods ,and lion

184 / *G Street Chronicles*

masks were standing like they were on the front line waiting on them. The young guard that had dove in the ditch had recovered and was reaching for the M-16 he had dropped trying to avoid the truck, but his efforts were cut short as two female Squad members stood over him and squeezed their triggers, sending AK bullets ripping through his body. The other guards opened fire on the Squad, but it seemed to only last for a second as the AKs returned fire from the Squad, sounding off like a drum roll and making quick work of the seven guards.

The warehouse boss wasted no time surrendering as he yelled from the warehouse, "Don't shoot, I'm unarmed." He put his hands out the door, hoping they would not get a shot off. The Squad quickly closed in, claiming their hostage.

Big Block and Blow made their way into the warehouse and their eyes got big like they were in a candy land. The warehouse was full of at least a hundred or more vehicles. There were Lambos, Ferraris, and a lot more cars they couldn't even pronounce. Big Block lifted the door on a red Lambo, and on the front seat was the key and a fresh, brand new title.

"Start that bitch up," Blow said. Block wasted no time putting the key in and the starting the car up. The pipes growled as he revved the engine.

"Yeah, this mu'fucka right," Block said, stepping out the car.

"Let's get to work," Blow yelled to the rest of the Squad

that were still standing outside the warehouse. The Squad members got right to business, opening up the warehouse doors so the other Squad members could drive the cars out of the warehouse and to their new homes. The rest of the Squad members were already in the next warehouse when Block and Blow entered.

"What the fuck!" Blow said as he looked around in amazement. The warehouse they were in was more like an armory. The only thing that was missing was a tank.

"Oh, it's most definitely going down!" Block said, watching the Squad members going to work loading the truck.

"You ain't never lied," Blow added as he picked up a rocket launcher out of a crate and put it on his shoulder.

* * * * *

The red haired casino boss passed the light-skinned armored car driver and grabbed a shotgun out of the closet. "You come with me," the casino boss said, lugging two oxygen tanks toward the safe. The heavy set armored car driver was ready for action as he pulled his .44 magnum from his holster.

"I assure you gentlemen, this will all be over with very shortly, and you will definitely be rewarded for helping," the red haired man said as he reached the door to the safe.

"You're right about that," the light-skin driver said right before cocking the shotgun and pulling the trigger, leaving red hair's and brains all over the wall. The other two casino security guards were caught completely caught off guard by Trouble's .44 magnum as he squeezed the trigger, sending bullets into his two targets, leaving them both dead before they even hit the floor.

"Damn, Trouble!" Goldie said, cocking the shotgun again. "Who the fuck is you, Desperado?"

"Hell yeah," Trouble responded, blowing the smoke that was coming out the tip of the gun like he was blowing out a birthday candle, and then spun the gun around his finger and put it back in his holster, imitating a cowboy.

"You won't be needing these," Trouble said, reaching down and grabbing the high powered machine guns out the hand of the two dead victims, and passing one to Goldie as they made their way toward the money room door. The four guards in the hall didn't even hear the gunshots from inside the money room that had claimed the boss and their colleague's lives. The door to the money room opened up, and out came Goldie and Trouble.

"Back-up's here!" Goldie yelled to the men who relaxed.

One even yelled, "About fucking time!" but that was the last word he said before the machine gun fire from Goldie and Trouble, and ripped into the four guards, leaving them dead as a doorknobs. Within seconds, the door to the casino where the Squad members were waiting buzzed open. The one standing on the table hit a button on his watch and yelled out, "Ten minutes!"

The Squad members jumped into action, emptying the safe of sixty million dollars and still had two minutes to spare as they loaded onto the tour bus and pulled out the parking lot driving right by the casinos back-up as they finally arrived.

When Tony got done telling The Bull what had happened, The Bull was furious, hitting the table so hard he knocked his glass of wine over onto his white suit and didn't even care. His rage was why they called him The Bull in the first place, and he was definitely seeing red. That was when his cell phone rang. Tony didn't even get a chance to answer it before The Bull had snatched it and answered it himself.

"What is it now?" he yelled into the phone, still in his rage.

"That's no way to answer the phone!" The caller responded.

"Who is this?" The Bull demanded, looking angrier.

"The owner of a brand new Lambo, that's who it is, you pasta eating mu'fucka!" Qwon said, laughing.

"You think this is a fucking game, you little monkey! I'm gonna see to it myself that you die a long, hard death. You have no idea who you're fucking with," The Bull responded.

"Oh, we know exactly who we're fucking with - the little angry man with the wine stain on his suit." Those words sent a chill down The Bull's spine.

Then, a knock came on the window of the pizza parlor, causing The Bull, Tony, and the two body guards to look.

Their bodies seemed to freeze once they saw the twins and Tish with their lion masks on, holding AKs with two hundred round drums on the bottom of them.

"It's a hit!" Tony yelled, but it was the last words that were said by anybody in the pizza parlor as the assassins squeezed the triggers, sending over five hundred rounds into the restaurant and leaving nothing behind but destruction and a bloody massacre of revenge. What a better day for it to happen, on Valentine's Day.

The city that was labeled the city of vision and wealth was a city under siege. The Beast had its grip on the city and it was becoming tighter and tighter as the days past. People that once looked down upon black people and their poverty stricken hoods were now everyday visitors to the hoods. They watched as bank accounts were wiped out, houses went into foreclosures, and car notes were left unpaid, leaving the bank business going down the hole fast. The rich area of the city where there was little crime was plagued with violence and theft, ripping the trust right out of their community. The Beast was turning them on each other.

Some people hadn't slept in weeks, doing whatever they had to do to supply their habits, while others crowded rehab centers begging for a cure that would never be found. The city was being devoured and the governor and mayor knew something had to be done immediately, especially with the media having a field day with what they called the second coming of the St. Valentine's Day massacre that left twenty-one dead and mob boss, Johnny The Bull Portelli, in the hospital with multiple gunshot wounds.

The chief of police had no choice but to call a meeting with all four police districts, because what they were up against was way bigger than anything they'd ever seen. The Beast was growing hungrier and hungrier, and it most definitely was feeding time. Even as the meeting was beginning, the police knew that for every second they wasted, another victim was lost.

"I'd like to thank you all for coming out tonight," the large, white man said. "I'm Chief Yager for those of you that don't know me," he said, pausing before continuing.

"You all know why we're here, so let's get down to business," he said while walking toward a bulletin board that had pictures of the Royal Family on it. "These are our targets!" he said, pointing toward the pictures. "These individuals before you are the ones we believe to be responsible for this drug that has taken over the city. We also have reason to believe that this so called St. Valentine's Day massacre is also their handy work. We're even reopening an investigation into the so called death of their father, Tyler Scott, also known as King, and the assassination of the SWAT team that was transporting him. At this point, we have no proof of nothing, but with all of us working together, we will take this family down once and for all. With that, I'd like to introduce Agent Fellows from the F.B.I. He will be leading this investigation."

Agent Fellows stood up in front of the auditorium full

of police and wasted no time getting to the point. "You may look at these twins and see that they're only sixteen, or look at their sister and see nothing more than a pretty face, but I assure you, ladies and gentlemen, what you're looking at is only an illusion. What you're really looking at are three cold blooded killers!" Those words seemed to echo over the silence filled room as he continued. "This will not be a walk in the park to bring them down because they're filthy rich and the people in the low income areas worship the ground they walk on. To us, they are nothing more than rich killers. To them, they're royalty. They even call the Marion Jones projects they live in the palace. If this sounds scary to you, they are mild compared to their father, who I have reason to believe is still alive and pulling all the strings behind this new drug that has taken over the streets. It's only a matter of time before they make a mistake, and that's when we'll be waiting. It's time we apply a little pressure, ladies and gentlemen, and see if we can force them into making a mistake," Fellows continued. Fellows knew he couldn't take King and his kids down alone, so he did what he thought was best—get his own army. As he looked over the room full of officers, he knew it was time for war.

* * * * * *

It was definitely a good day in the hood, but for it to be the hood, it sure didn't look like it anymore. With the drugs gone for almost a month, the black people were given a second chance to live life. The only tears were tears of joy, especially since the money taken from the casino was put back in the community, or what they called the kingdom. For once, the blacks were trusting each other and helping each other. They saw that the drugs that plagued the community was nothing more than the trick of the enemy that kept them fighting against each other over the years. The sun was most definitely shining on the hood, but the sun wasn't the only thing shining in the hood.

The Royal Family and the Goon Squad put the vehicles they took in the warehouse heist to good use. It was something like a dream to see young blacks riding one hundred to three hundred thousand dollar cars up and down the project streets with no envy for one another. Hustling together had everybody's pockets swollen; even the lowest man on the totem pole was making at least two thousand dollars a week. With the two projects added, the family's take was somewhere around twenty million a week, and rapidly increasing by the day.

The only people that weren't smiling in the hood were Officer Nash and his partner, Brooks. They were the neighborhood jump out boys, not to mention they were also as dirty as they came; extortion, bribery, planting evidence, you name it, they did it. They took pride in putting fear in the hood, using their power to their advantage to control people or destroy people, whichever came first. Lately, they'd been real aggravated; the operation that was running down in the projects was way over their heads. They couldn't catch anybody dirty. By the time they even got close to the hood, they were spotted and reported by lookouts, and by the time they even got close to the projects, everything was shut down. They were usually able to get a dope fein' to tell something, but with the dope out of their systems and the Royal Family taking care of them, they couldn't get information out of anybody. They couldn't do anything but sit back as the candy red Bentley pulled up in the parking lot of the projects.

"I can't believe this shit!" Nash said to his partner. "These pieces of shit riding in cars worth more than my house."

"Shit, your house and mine put together," Brooks responded, sipping his coffee.

The doors of the Bentley opened up and Nash wasted no time putting the Crown Vic they were in into drive and hitting the lights. Within seconds, they were behind the Bentley with the lights flashing and guns drawn.

"Let me see your fucking hands!" Brooks yelled to Qwon and Trouble, who were laughing as they put they hands up.

"What is this, valet?" Qwon yelled at the officers. Nash walked right up behind him and put his gun to the back of Qwon's head.

"You got anymore jokes?" Nash asked.

"Yeah, have you heard the one about the two homosexual cops named Brooks and Nash?" Qwon said, causing him and Trouble to laugh.

Nash and Brooks weren't little punk ass cops. Nash was

about two hundred and forty five pounds, about six-two, and all muscle with sandy blonde hair. Brooks was about six three, and two hundred and sixty pounds with brown hair, and to most people they were very intimidating. That was why they couldn't believe that even with a gun on the back of their heads, the boys showed no sign of fear or panic. Nash wanted to pull the trigger so bad, but he thought to himself another time another place. He put his gun up and pushed Qwon on the car, searching him.

"Ten percent is gonna be our cut, or your little operation down here is gonna suffer greatly, especially when my partner and I start hauling everybody that even looks like y'all to jail on fucked up charges!" Nash said, turning Qwon around looking him in his eyes.

"Shit, that's all y'all want is ten percent?" Qwon asked, pausing before continuing. "I was thinking about giving and your partner way more than that." Nash definitely liked the sound of that.

"I'm listening," he said with a grin on his face. "How about I give y'all one hundred percent of fuck you and suck my dick, and you and your partner can split it 50/50," Qwon said, grinning at the officer.

"Yeah, laugh now and we'll see who's laughing in the end!" Nash said, walking toward the police car.

"Let's go, partner. We'll most definitely see you two later!" Brooks added, getting into the car with his partner. Nash pulled the Crown Vic out of the parking lot full of anger and humiliation, knowing he had lost this little battle, but he would win the war.

Later on that night, the Family was in Goldie's apartment having a smoke session and still talking about the incident earlier with Nash and Brooks when there was a knock at the door. Goldie put his glass of Remy down and grabbed his Glock 40 off the table, not willing to take any chances. The knocks came harder and louder as he approached the door. He looked through the peephole at the hooded individual on the other side. Goldie gripped his gun tighter while trying to make out who the visitor was.

"Who is it?" Goldie yelled through the door, causing the person to look up at the peephole, exposing the long scar that was on the side his face and covered his eyes.

The twins, Tish, and Trouble were all on point, ready for anything as Goldie turned the lock open with one hand while his other hand held the gun to the door, aiming directly at the individual. The click sound was followed by a few words from the other side of the door. What Goldie didn't know was that these words brought a message of death with them.

"It's Grimey!" That was what Goldie heard as he finished opening up the door, pulling it open slowly.

"What up, little nigga?" Goldie said, letting his guard down now that he had recognized one of the Squad members.

"It's going down, Goldie!" Grimey said, almost out of breath.

"Come inside!" Goldie said, peeping out in the hallway and looking both ways, making sure everything was everything, and then closing the door and getting to what Grimey was talking about

"Now what's going down?" Grimey took his hood off and looked at who all was in the apartment before he spoke, knowing all eyes were on him and what he had to say was about to effect someone in the room.

"Lil' Chris!"

"What about Lil' Chris?" Trouble asked.

"They killed him!" Those words seemed to take the air out of the room and all the attention shifted from Grimey to Trouble, who was standing up with a concerned look on his face, especially since Lil' Chris was his little brother.

* * * * *

The Bull couldn't wait to recover from the single gunshot wound he received from the so called Valentine's Day massacre. He knew if it wasn't for Tony diving in front of him when the shooting started, he probably would've ended up with way more than a bullet hole in his upper chest and Tony's brains splashed all over his face. The thought still sent a chill down his spine as he sat on the side of his hospital bed. He was so deep in his thoughts, he almost didn't hear his two body guards that were sitting outside his room had opened the room door to check on him.

"You alright, boss?" the huge, bald headed man asked.

The Bull just waived him off.

He refused to show a sign of weakness. He waited for the door to close before clicking his morphine button to relieve some of his pain. He was getting ready to lay back down when he was interrupted again by the door coming open, and that time he spoke out. "I said I was a'right!" he yelled.

"Mr. Portelli?" the nurse said, peeping her head in.

"I'm sorry," The Bull said. "Come on in."

"How you doing, Mr. Portelli?" she asked, pushing her cart around the bed and giving him a smile that could light up a room.

"I was a little edgy, but I'm doing much better now that you're here," he said, flirting.

"I bet you say that to all the nurses," se said, flirting back while she opened the drawers on her cart, pulling her supplies out to take The Bull's blood. She grabbed his arm, checking for his veins as she kept talking.

"You've been through a lot for such a sweet man," she said, locating his vein. "Here we go right here. This will only take a second." She grabbed the needle off her cart and opening the package it was in, but she dropped it on the floor. "Damn, you got me all nervous, I hope I got another needle with me," she said, picking up the needle off the floor and taking it in the bathroom to dispose of it.

"Take your time, sweetheart!" The Bull said, watching her from behind as she walked across the room to the hazard box to get rid of the useless needle. He thought, *Damn, she's fine as hell especially those hypnotizing brown eyes.*

"I'm so sorry, Mr. Portelli!" she said from the bathroom, turning the light off in the bathroom and coming out, and making her way back across the room to her cart . The Bulls eye's watched her every step, hoping she messed up again. "I'm just a little nervous, I've never been around a famous person before," she said, bending down looking through her cart for another needle.

"I'm far from famous, sweetheart," The Bull said, being modest as his ego would allow.

"Sure you are!" she said, laughing, still rummaging through her cart. "I saw you on the news—they said you were some kind of mob boss."

"Sweetheart, don't believe what you see on TV. It's always more to a story than what they tell you. I'm merely a victim of a random shooting."

"Damn, I don't have any little needles left. I hope you're not afraid of a big one?"

"I'm a big boy, I'm sure I can handle it," he replied, still staring at her ass.

"I'm not one to believe everything I hear on TV. You're right, it's always more to a story than they tell," she said pausing. She stood up with her back still to him as she continued what she was saying.

"If I was them, I would've talked about the real things you are famous for, the guns, cars, and the drugs, or how about the kids you tried to have killed outside the club a few weeks ago!" The Bull couldn't believe what he was hearing coming from his nurse.

"What w…what?" he said, stuttering as panic filled his body, ready to scream for his security with his next breath.

"Calm down, Mr. Portelli, this will all be over with soon," she said, turning around. "This won't hurt that much, we're just gonna take a little blood. Trust me, it'll all be over with before you know it." The Bull's eyes showed the terror of a child about to get a shot from a doctor for the first time, except the needle in her hand was a .45 automatic with a silencer on it.

"Who…who are you?" he stuttered out, finding himself staring in her brown eyes again.

"Let's just say I'm a concerned parent that always cleans up after my kids!" Those were the last words The Bull ever heard as the nurse squeezed the trigger, sending five hollow tips into his chest and two more splitting his face open. Just like she came, she packed her stuff and pushed her cart out the door where the bodyguards were waiting. "All done in there, you gentlemen have a nice day," she said. They didn't respond, it probably had something to do with the bullets she put in their head on the way in the room. She just laughed as she walked down the hallway pushing her cart.

* * * * *

The death of Lil' Chris took the hood by storm and left a most definite effect on those that lived there, not to mention

Trouble and his family. Chris had only been in the ground two days, and the memory of the night Trouble had to identify his brother was stuck in his mind.

The streets were covered with people, police, and ambulances. The yellow tape blocked off the alley where the body was found. One of the officers flagged him in the tape toward a body that was covered with a white sheet. The closer he got, the faster his heart beat. The officer turned toward Trouble as they stood over the body.

"Sir, I know this is hard, but I need you to identify the body we have here, so do the best you can." Trouble didn't know what he meant by that, but he was about to find out. When the officer told his partner to pull the sheet back, it was like in slow motion, unveiling a gruesome sight that Trouble could barely make out as a face at first. The face of the victim had been so badly beaten, it looked as if there were no bones left in it.

"Do you know this person?" the officer asked.

Trouble didn't even hear him or anything else around him. His eyes focused harder, not on the face that showed no identity, but what gave Trouble the answer to the question that would change his life. It was the chain around the neck of the victim. It was a white gold chain with a diamond covered "C" on the charm that he had bought for his brother. All he remembered next was the screams of his mother and sister as they answered the officer's question.

What happened next that night was crazy. The police had

witnesses that said a black, unmarked police car pulled up in the alley, and Nash and Brooks got out and pulled Chris out the backseat and left him there dead. Once the word got out, the people went crazy, throwing bottles and rocks at the police and their cars. The police had to call the riot control, but it only made matters worse. By the time they got things under control by shooting gas in the crowd, police cars were turned over and on fire, and at least five police were rushed to the hospital with injuries.

The people in the hood were fed up, and the death of Lil' Chris seemed to spark the fire that brought them all together. The funeral for Lil' Chris was one for the record books. It looked more like the million man march. There were people from everywhere that came to show their support and to protest why the two officers weren't arrested yet. It took a week for the two officers to be arrested, and even then they were given a signature bond. The protesters were all hoping that all that would change at the pretrial hearing.

"Trouble, you good?" Qwon asked, giving Trouble a nudge and breaking his train of thought.

"Yeah, I'm cool," Trouble replied, realizing he had zoned off for a minute in the courtroom while waiting on the two officers to come in. The courtroom was like a scene from an old racist movie, in which the blacks sat on one side and the whites sat on the other; except instead of the blacks and whites, it was the Squad and the police. The tension was definitely in the air as both sides gave dirty looks back and forth at each other. When the two officers finally walked in with their lawyer, the courtroom erupted, but both sides maintained their composure.

When the bailiff yelled, "All rise!" you could barely hear him over the chants of, "Fuck the police!" that rumbled through the courtroom from outside.

"The Honorable Judge Tillman presiding, you may all be seated!"

"Judge Tillman!" Twon said. "Why does that sound familiar?" he asked Mr. Clayton, who thought it would be best to chaperon his clients.

"He's the judge that got that fake warrant against your father and sent him to jail. He's as crooked as they come!" Qwon couldn't believe what he heard as he looked at the judge's stern face. The judge took his seat and began the court hearing. The lawyer of the cops stood up and quickly began talking.

"Your Honor, I ask that all charges be dropped against my clients. This is clearly the word of a drug addict against the word of two outstanding officers of our community that work in the worse area in the city. The witnesses have also been arrested by my clients on numerous drug charges as well as prostitution!" The things said about the witnesses were the truth, but nobody cared that the witnesses were off the drugs and wasn't prostituting anymore, and the D.A quickly made that understood.

"Your Honor, the state agrees with the defense on this,

we don't have enough evidence to proceed and our witness is not credible."

The judge jumped in like he was given his que and the scene was all rehearsed. "I see no reason to waste anymore of the court's time. Case dismissed. The defendants are free to go!" he said, and then slammed his gavel down.

The cheer from the police officers side of the courtroom was like a slap in the face to the Squad, but like well-trained soldiers, the Royal Family stood up and walked out the courtroom, and the Squad followed right behind without even saying a word. The officers, on the other hand, taunted the Squad on their way out, embracing their victory. The scene outside the courthouse was chaos, angry protesters shouting and yelling. The police were in there riot gear and had sealed off the courthouse stairs as the two officers made their way out of the courtroom surrounded by cops that escorted them to the black limo that was waiting for them. Once safe inside, Nash and Brooks looked at each other and started laughing as the limo sped down the street.

The riot squad thought the blacks were definitely gonna riot, but to their surprise, the exact opposite happened. The people were actually laughing and smiling as they dispersed like it was some kind of inside joke or something. The riot commander couldn't believe it was the same group of people that was just yelling, "Fuck the police!"

Nash passed his partner a drink he had made from the bar in the back of the limo. "To crime and punishment!" Brook said, toasting with his partner.

"To crime and punishment!" Nash replied, and then he smelled something that he knew very well from being a cop.

"You smell weed?"

"Yeah, I do smell weed!" Brooks said, sniffing the air.

Nash looked out the window and noticed they weren't going toward the police station. They were going in the opposite direction, and in the distance, he could see the buildings of the Marion Jones approaching. Before the two officers could say anything, the limo's privacy glass went down and let out a cloud of weed smoke. When the weed smoke cleared, there was Blow with a blunt in his mouth driving, and Big Block turned around facing them, holding two Tecks in his hands aimed at Nash and Brooks, wishing they'd move so he could kill them.

"To crime and punishment!" Blow said, blowing the weed smoke out, almost coughing.

"Yeah, crime and punishment, I like that shit!" Big Block added, laughing with Blow.

The look on the officers' faces truly showed that they weren't expecting the situation they were in , especially since they paid Judge Tillman fifty thousand dollars to throw the case out, and now they were in the back of a limo looking down the barrel of two guns as they pulled up in the project's parking lot.

"Welcome to our kingdom, mu'fuckas!" Big Block said

as he continued to laugh at the officers.

Nobody would've guessed that the scene outside the courthouse was really a diversion for a kidnapping. There was no way two white cops were going to jail for killing a black boy on the word of an ex-junkie. The judicial system protected its gang at all cost, and it was even easier to do that when you had crooked judges like Tillman, who was working late in his chambers as usual when he heard a knock on the door. The judge put his drink down on his desk, standing up to go answer the door. *It must be the janitor telling me he's leaving,* he thought, and then he heard words from the other side of the door.

"You got court in five minutes."

Court? he thought. *The courthouse has been closed for four hours now.* He hated playing games and he was angry as he snatched the door open, ready to give whomever it was a piece of mind, but his idea quickly changed when he found himself looking down the barrel of Red's .357. Red grabbed the frightened judge by his collar and led him down the hallway until they reached the door to his courtroom.

"You won't get away with this, I'm a judge!" the judge said.

"Not today, mu'fucka!" Red replied, opening the door with the judge's face.

What the judge saw next scared him more than the gun in Red's hand. Nash and Brooks were trying their best not to panic as they sat handcuffed to their chairs in a room that was completely covered from the ceiling to the floor in plastic, which in their eyes was not good. When the room door opened, their hearts almost jumped out their chest. Goldie walked in and closed the door behind him, dumping ashes from the blunt he was smoking on the plastic covered floor.

"We can do this the easy way or the hard way," Goldie said, pausing as he blew weed smoke in Nash and Brook's faces.

"I'm gonna ask y'all some questions, and y'all gonna answer me, ya dig?" The officer's didn't say anything, they just stared at Goldie as he continued. "What do the police buddies have planned?" Goldie said. The officers still chose to give him the silent treatment. "So, y'all want us to snitch on each other, but y'all don't want to, huh? Ain't that some shit!" Goldie said, laughing to himself. "I'm trying to help y'all, but y'all gotta help me! Now, what's going down?" Goldie said, pausing. "That sounds like y'all don't it? Now, all I need is a crazy partner!" When he said that, the noise from the other side of the door sent chills up the officers' spine.

"Judge Tillman, what a pleasure to see you again. What's it been, ten years!" King said, sitting in the judge's seat in the courtroom. Judge Tillman was speechless as he was escorted to his seat at the defendant's table next to his court appointed lawyer.

"I'm gonna be representing you, so sit back and let me handle this shit, I personally know the D.A," Qwon said, looking at the D.A. table where Twon was sitting, giving him the finger. "See, that means we're in good shape!" Qwon said, laughing. Judge Tillman didn't know what was happening to him. He'd never been on that side of the bench before, but he could now see through the eyes of so many blacks he'd sent away.

"Order in the court!" King said, pausing. "Today, we're here to bring charges against Judge Tillman for conspiracy to destroy a family and basically being a bitch ass mu'fucka. How does the defendant plead?"

"Not guilty, Your Honor. It's clear that my client is a pussy ass mu'fucka, and not a bitch ass mu'fucka," Qwon said.

"I object, Your Honor!" Twon said, jumping up from his seat. "Anybody that looks like him has to be a bitch ass mu'fucka!" King had to stop himself from laughing. The only one that wasn't laughing was Judge Tillman, who looked confused as hell.

Qwon turned to the Judge Tillman and said, "I don't think we're gonna win this case, the D.A. is actually smarter than he looks."

"Now that I've heard both arguments, has the jury come up with a verdict?" King said, looking over at Tish in the jury box.

"I have come to a decision," Tish said, standing up. "Guilty on all charges!"

"Judge Tillman, you've been found guilty. Is there anything you'd like to say before sentencing?" King asked.

Judge Tillman couldn't believe what was happening as

he stood up and started talking.

"Please, let me go. I have a family!" he said before King cut him off.

"Do you know how many people stood before you that had a family that needed them, but to you, they were nothing more than another nigga, fuck'em! Ten years ago, you sat where I'm at and gave me life with no chance of parole." King paused, grinning with those gold teeth the same way he did when Judge Tillman had sentenced him. Tillman had been haunted by that smile for many years, and there it was again. "I hereby sentence you to death!" Judge Tillman tried to raise his hands and tried to beg as Red approached with his .357.

"Wait, please!" was all he got to say as Red raised his gun and pulled the trigger, putting a bullet right between Judge Tillman's eyes that knocked him back in his chair and left a gaping hole out of the back of his head.

"Damn, Unk, you got his brains all on my shirt!" Qwon said.

"Better his than yours" Red replied, laughing.

Goldie made his way toward the room door and started turning the knob, looking back at the officers, whose tough faces were showing signs of fear, hoping that the sound on the other side of the door wasn't what they thought it was. "I tried to help y'all, let's see if my partner can get anything out of y'all," Goldie said, opening the door and letting his partner in. The officers' eyes got big when they saw Trouble come in with a chainsaw in his hands.

"Scream if y'all change your mind!" Goldie said, yelling over the buzzing of the chainsaw, and then he closed the door.

The officers quickly changed the quiet routine and began pleading that they'd talk, but Trouble played deaf and wasted no time putting the chainsaw on Brook's shoulder. In seconds, his arm was on the floor, still handcuffed at the wrist. Brook's screamed so loud, Nash pissed on himself knowing he was next.

"Wait wai..."Nash tried to say when the chainsaw ripped into his knee, grinding through it with ease until it was no longer connected to his body. Trouble couldn't think of nothing but how they killed his brother. He stood there and laughed at the screams of pain as their blood covered the plastic.

* * * * *

Six murders in two days sent the city into a frenzy. The Bull and two of his body guards found dead at the hospital, Judge Tillman found dead in his courtroom, and the worse one of all was the two duffle bags found in the mayor's office that contained the body parts of officers Nash and Brooks. The message was clear and simple, nobody was out of the reach of the Family. Even though there were no witnesses, there was none needed because everybody knew who was responsible for the deaths and why. The racial tension was everywhere. The blacks glorified the twins and Tish like heroes while the whites that weren't in the belly of The Beast and most of the police wanted them dead!

The racial conflict rose among the police as well. The black cops were standing up for their people, but it was still those black cops that wished they were born white that were staying on the side with the whites. The underdog was definitely on top and the city knew it. The best thing would have been for the mayor to put in a call for help, but he refused to lose his city to a bunch of hoods, and he made that clear to the chief of police, who was given strict instructions to eliminate the threat to the city by any means necessary. By the commands he gave his officers, it was time for business.

"Our targets are considered armed and extremely dangerous!" the chief said, pausing and making eye contact with the officers in the room before continuing. "They have no mercy for law enforcement. They will kill you, so I got one thing to say - shoot first, ask questions later. Now, let's suit up and get these mu'fuckas!" he said, walking out the briefing room with his troops close behind.

Agent Fellows was no longer running the operation. It was personal since they killed two of their officers. There was no way the family was gonna make it out those projects alive the chief thought as an evil grin covered his face.

It was eight a.m., only thirty minutes since the chief finished briefing his officers, and the caravan of at least fifty police vehicles made its way through the city, with two helicopters overhead with swat members in them. The cars all had the lights on, but no sirens in order to surprise the targets, but they were about to get a surprise of their own.

* * * * *

Benny had been laying low since Juicy got killed, knowing he'd most definitely be next. With the family at war with the police and The Bull dead, it was time for him to escape the city for a while. The best move would be to let the police and the Family kill themselves off, then he would return and take his city back. He was thinking to himself while he packed his bags in his bedroom at his penthouse. He was almost finished when he heard the door to the penthouse open and close. *It must be Silk*, he thought to himself since he'd gone to get the car.

* * * * *

"Silk, you ready? Just think, in a few more hours we're gonna be in the air on our way to the Bahamas!" Benny said, but he got no response. "Silk, you hear me?"

Benny knew he could hear somebody walking around in the other room. He wasn't taking any chances, so he quickly grabbed his .38 snub nose off the bed and turned toward the room door, and that was when he heard what sounded like a bowling ball come rolling across the floor and into his bedroom, stopping at the bottom of his feet. Only, it wasn't a bowling ball, it was Silk's head.

* * * * *

With the Marion Jones projects in view, the adrenalin was pumping through the officers, anger and rage only fueled their fire. Usually, the hood and its surrounding areas were busy, but that morning was just the opposite. It was if they'd drove into a ghost town. Nobody was outside, even the little stores were closed. The officers couldn't believe what they saw, but it was too late to turn back, especially since they had arrived in front of the projects.

"They're here!" Twon said to Goldie, who was on the other end of the phone he was talking into.

"Fa sho, nigga. We watching these bitches right now. They ain't gonna know what hit them!" Goldie replied, and then hung up. He turned to Trouble, who was in the car with him watching the police. "Look at these dumb mu'fuckas, they ain't got a fucking clue what's about to happen!" He paused, turning to Big Block, who was in the back with Blow. "Call the Squad and tell them it's a green light." The police had definitely made a big mistake Trouble thought, putting on his lion mask.

"Let's do this shit!" Trouble said, opening his car door with his AK-47 in hand. He watched the four bus loads full of Squad members that pulled up in the police station parking lot. The projects had been evacuated by the Family, only leaving behind the twins, Tish , and Uncle Red to take on the police force that was in front of the projects, preparing for their invasion of the second building where the twins' last known address was. It seemed to be a one sided battle with all the SWAT teams and police surrounding the area, but you couldn't tell by the calmness in the apartment as the Family got ready for war. The Family most definitely had their game faces on.

"It's time!" Red said, looking at his niece and nephews, knowing it could be the last time he'd see any of them alive. "Qwon, you go with me, Twon, you and Tish. We got twelve floors to cover, we'll take the upper floors, y'all take the lower. Now, let's show these bitches what the Family is made of!" Red paused.

"Family!"

"Family!"

"Family!"

"Family!" the twins and Tish repeated after their uncle.

Outside, the officers' confidence was high. They couldn't wait to drag the bodies of the twins and their sister out as the SWAT team commander gave his final instructions. "I want unit one to take the stairs and unit two in the elevator, unit three will be coming in from the roof. I want everybody on the sixth floor and our targets eliminated within ten minutes. Do you understand me?"

"Yes sir!" they all said.

"Well, let's get it done then!" the SWAT commander said, sending his troops into action. The streets were covered with police cars and cops with their guns drawn, aiming at the buildings as they watched the SWAT team enter the building.

* * * * *

Benny almost jumped out his skin looking at Silk's head at his feet. He let off six shots from his .38, trying to scare whomever it was, but he knew anybody crazy enough to cut somebody's head off surely wasn't scared of some warning shots. He wasted no time going in his closet and pulling his M-16 with the beam on it out and cocking it. "You think you can come in my place and kill me? Well, come on, mu'fuckas!"Benny said, and then squeezed off some rounds through the wall into the next room. "What you waiting on, come on in here!" Benny yelled out to the other room. He heard a sick laugh that he knew could only belong to one person. Then, the lights went out.

Once inside the building, the SWAT team moved quickly. The ten members of team one hit the stairs, leaving the other eight members of team two in the elevator. The helicopter had pulled over the top of the building and two ropes fell down from each side of it, allowing the eight SWAT members to slide down and gain access to the building from the roof.

"Go, go, go!" the team leader said, sending four men down to the roof while the others waited for the area to be secure, but something was definitely wrong as the first SWAT member hit the roof. Sharp pains went through every nerve in his feet, when he looked down, he couldn't believe what he saw.

The elevator had hit the third floor and they knew once they hit the sixth floor, they'd be on their own until the other two units reached them. The elevator had passed the fifth floor and they didn't know what would be waiting on them on the other side of the door, but they were ready as the elevator slowed down, reaching its destination. Their nerves were on the edge and the adrenalin was pumping as they took aim at the door. It was too bad they never heard the top hatch on the elevator open up.

The stairway was dim as SWAT made its way in between the third and fourth floor, and then a noise caused the team leader to hold his hand up, causing his unit to pause.

"You hear something?" he whispered to the man behind him, who didn't get a chance to response before two grenades came flying from around the corner and landing where SWAT was. "Grenade!" the leader yelled, but it was too late for anybody to escape. The grenade explosion seemed to shake the building, making easy work of the SWAT team, but Twon didn't take any chances as he popped from around the corner with his AK-47 and pulled the trigger.

The officer's screams of pain couldn't even explain the feeling he had as he saw the nine inch nails that stuck through his feet. The roof had been covered with a layer of plywood with nails coming through it. There was a small walk way through all the nails, but none of the officers saw it as the other three men hit the nails. One officer lost his balance, falling forward and sending nails ripping through his hands and knees while trying to stop his fall. The SWAT leader couldn't believe what he saw, and just when he thought things couldn't get any worse, the door to the rooftop flew open and there was Qwon standing there holding his Carbon 15 with two hands taking aim and squeezing the trigger, sending bullets slicing through the officers like razor blades, ripping them open. The SWAT team in the helicopter returned fire, trying to save the officers that were trapped on the roof, but it was too late, they were already dead. Qwon turned the Carbine on the helicopter and returned fire, leaving them no choice but to retreat or have the helicopter ripped open along with them.

The elevator was silent as they waited for the doors to open, but the doors seemed to be stuck. The officers lowered their weapons as two of them tried to pry the door open with their hands. That would turn out to be there first and last mistake. The female laughter from above them caused them all to look up as the latch opened. They attempted to aim toward the ceiling, but Tish never gave them a chance to get a shot off. The bullets from her AK rained on their heads, leaving a flood of blood and dead bodies.

With the penthouse completely dark, Benny moved slowly out of his bedroom, holding his M-16 tightly with his finger nervously on the trigger. "King, I know you there!" he yelled, but there was no response. "Come on, King, I thought we were friends! I know you're not still mad at me after all these years. Come on, I'm sorry. I even got a gift for you!"

Benny said, then pulled the M-16 trigger, waiving it across the darkness in front of him and spraying the penthouse with bullets. The muzzle flash lit the room, but he didn't see King anywhere. "What you hiding for?" Benny yelled into the darkness, but once again, he didn't get a response. "Fuck this hide and seek shit, let's talk face to face like men!"

"I was thinking the same thing," King replied, sending chill's down Benny's spine, especially since King was standing face to face with him. Benny didn't know how King got so close without him hearing him, but it was too late to worry about that. King threw an uppercut that landed with so much force, it almost flipped him completely over. It left him unconscious before he even hit the floor.

The police were definitely losing the battle with the family. They had four men down on the roof and lost all communication with the other two teams. The chief was in a frenzy as he paced back and forth, trying to get his thoughts together. Even with around seventy officers positioned around the building, the chief wasn't taking any more chances. He got on the radio. "Headquarters, I need all available units to the Marion Jones housing immediately. Over!" The chief stood there holding his radio waiting on a response, but nobody responded.

"Headqaurters! This is the chief of police, respond!" That time, he got what he wanted.

"This headquarters, mu'fucka, what is your fucking emergency?" The chief couldn't believe what he heard.

"Who is this?" he demanded, yelling into his radio.

"Who is you? You called us!" Blow responded. The chief was at a loss for words, but he couldn't help but listen as the new dispatcher was talking to someone else.

"Aw, it's some mu'fucka on here talking about the chief!" Blow said to Big Block, who took over as dispatcher.

"What up, chief?" Block asked, blowing smoke out from the blunt he smoked.

"Whoever this is, you are in a lot of trouble!" the chief responded, not knowing what else to say.

"Yeah, yeah, I've heard that before. Sounds like you're the one in trouble calling for back-up." Block paused, hitting his blunt again before continuing. "I'd love to keep talking to you, but I hate talking to a dead man!" The chief looked at his radio, confused by the last words he'd just heard. He couldn't help but think to himself that going down there was a mistake. It was too bad for him that he wasn't the only one thinking that.

Red had been listening to the scanner, using the conversation the chief had over the radio to find his target in the crowd of police below, and his plan worked perfectly. He took aim with his sniper rifle from a tenth story window and squeezed the trigger, sending a bullet smashing into the side of the chief's head, almost knocking it off his shoulders. The surrounding officers wasted no time opening fire on the building, sending bullets ripping through the building's walls and windows. The gunfire seemed to last for almost five minutes as officers squeezed their triggers until their clips were empty. By the time the gunfire stopped, gun smoke was like fog in the air and the face of the building was riddled with bullet holes. The officers watched the building closely for any movement, and that was when someone with a bullhorn began speaking.

"Put your guns down. We have you surrounded, there is no way you can escape. If you cooperate, nobody will be hurt!" The officers were used to hearing that speech, the only difference was it was coming from Tish, who was on the roof of the building standing on the edge with her bullhorn in one hand and her AK in the other. Within seconds, the twins made their way down the path in between the nails and joined their sister. The officers couldn't believe what they saw but what happened next was even more amazing to them.

The officers couldn't help but look around at the surroundings, the same surroundings that showed no sign of life on their way in was full of life as the residents of the hood seemed to come out of nowhere, quickly filling the streets from every direction armed with firearms, ready to die for their kingdom. The streets were like a standoff. The police did their best to try and cover in every direction, ready for the gun battle that could start at any second with the wrong move. Even being surrounded by almost one thousand armed black men and women, the police looked ready to accept the challenge. The tension was so thick you could see it. The stares from both sides showed no sign of weakness, then suddenly, everything changed as one officer set off a chain reaction that would never be forgotten. Everything seemed to be going in slow motion as he dropped his gun and put his hands up. One by one, the officers followed his lead. Instantly, the cheers of victory filled the air. Tish and the twins had taken over the city. Red watched from the doorway of the rooftop, knowing that it was only the beginning for his niece and nephews. They had won the battle, but the war would be the true test, and Red planned to have them ready for the war of their lives when the time presented itself, but not even Red's warlike mentality and cold heart could hide how proud he was. When his niece and nephews turned around, his golden smile showed and told it all.

For a moment, Benny didn't remember what had just happened to him as he began waking up from being knocked out, but he was quickly reminded when he felt the pain in his face. Still groggy, he couldn't believe he was still alive as he made his way up on his wobbly legs, then suddenly the lights came on and what Benny saw next made his heart skip a beat. King was standing there by the door with a Desert Eagle in his hand aimed at Benny.

"Please, King, don't kill me!" Benny pleaded, putting his hands up. "I'll give you money, whatever you want, plea…" But, Benny never got to finish his words. King shot Benny a look that could kill, but that wasn't what stopped Benny from talking, it was the grin on King's face that was followed by him putting his gun in his waistline, and turning around and walking out that left Benny speechless. Benny couldn't believe what had just happened, but he was just happy to be alive. He gave a loud sigh of relief, trying to catch his breath, but he quickly realized it wasn't his breathing he heard. Benny slowly turned around as the fear of what he saw filled his body. Benny looked as if he'd seen a ghost as his eyes could see what was sitting on his bed in the room behind him, watching his every move. Benny didn't even realize he was pissing on himself. He was numb from fear, his legs seemed to be stuck in cement as he watched the lion climb off the bed, walking toward him.

King had reached the elevator, stepped inside, and waited on the doors to close when he heard the mighty roar of the lion and the screams of pain from Benny.

"Kiiing!" Benny screamed, but King only laughed as the elevator doors shut, taking him to the garage. When the doors opened, he stepped out in the dock garage and almost simultaneously, a black van came speeding his way, stopping right in front of him. King grabbed the door handle and pulled the door open, looking at the driver before hopping in and closing the door behind him.

"Where to?" the driver asked.

"How about we go get our kids? We definitely got a lot of explaining to do," King replied, looking deep into the brown eyes of his Queen.

"We most definitely do," Queen replied as she pulled the van out of the garage and headed to the Marion Jones.

Enjoy a bonus read

from

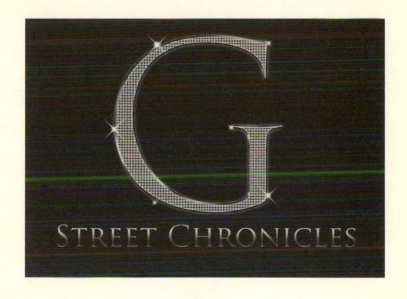

Visit www.gstreetchronicles.com
to view all our titles

Join us on Facebook
G Street Chronicles Fan Page

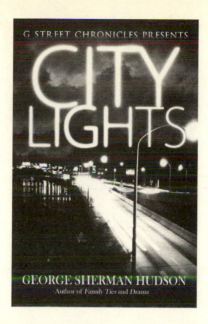

Lies, deceit and murder ran rampant throughout the city of Atlanta. Real and his lady, Constance, were living in the lap of luxury, with fancy cars, expensive clothes and a million dollar home until someone close to them alerted the feds to their illegal activity.

At the blink of an eye their perfect life was turned upside down. Just as Real was sorting things out on the home front, the head of Miami's most powerful Cartel gave him an ultimatum that would eventually force him back into the life he had swore off forever. Knowing this lifestyle would surely put Constance in danger, he made plans to send her away until the score was settled but things spiraled out of control. Now Real and Constance are in a fight for survival where friends become enemies and murder is essential. Atlanta's underworld to Miami's most affluent community—no stone was left unturned as Real fought to keep Constance safe while attempting to regain control of the lifestyle he once would kill for.

From the city of Atlanta to the cell block of Georgia's most dangerous prison, life under the City Lights would never be the same.

Chapter 1

The federal agent watched Real get out of his lime green Lamborghini Murcialago LP 460 with his fiancée Constance and head into G-Spot, his high class strip club located on Peachtree Street in downtown Atlanta. Real had been under federal investigation now for six months, ever since a federal informant tipped them off about his illegal activities.

Anyone who came into contact with Real would surely put him well beyond his actual age of only twenty-seven years. He was six feet tall with a medium built muscular frame that the ladies couldn't get enough of. His smooth, charcoal black skin, wavy hair, and light brown eyes gave him an exotic look that would have any woman fawning over him.

Real was a real charmer and a ladies man. He prided himself on his slick tongue and convincing rhetoric. Some people in the past had mistaken his easygoing manner for weakness, but in the end, they found out Real was an extremely dangerous individual.

Constance, Real's baby girl, fiancée, and business partner, was always by his side. Constance was three years older than Real, the spitting image of Lisa Raye with a little more hips and ass. Constance grew up in the College Park projects, where she got down with the grimiest of niggas hustling crack to the project fiends. After a few run-ins with other hustlers, the word spread quickly that lil' fine ass Constance would bust her gun at the drop of a dime.

After graduating from Banneker High, Constance tried her hand at real estate. In no time, she became a highly reputable broker that only dealt in the most high-end homes. Constance became a millionaire virtually overnight.

Constance and Real had met three years earlier at a mutual friend's birthday party. They kept each other company throughout the party. Before leaving the party, they exchanged numbers and promised to stay in contact. A week later, Constance was selling Real a $4.7 million estate in North Atlanta—the one in which they now both reside.

Real was a millionaire in his own right, raking in millions in the drug trade, more than he would ever make going legit. He supplied dealers from every coast. Moving over 100 kilos a week enabled him to live the lifestyle of some of the world's biggest sports figures. After continuous preaching from Constance to put together some kind of legit source of income, he opened up G-Spot, an upscale strip club that catered to the rich and famous.

Real and Constance were on their way to a Tyler Perry play when Real got a call from Max. "Say, cuz," said the manager of G-Spot, "we need your assistance down here. It's very important," Max said firmly.

Max was Real's older cousin. He was discharged from the military right after the Gulf War. As soon as Max heard about his lil' cousin Real starting a strip club, he practically begged him for the managing position. Constance was totally against it, but Real disregarded Constance's wishes and gave his cousin the job anyway. Unfortunately, it took a while for Real to see just how right Constance was.

"I'm on my way," Real said, placing his phone back into the car charger.

"On your way? Where you goin'?" Constance snapped.

"Max needs me down at the club. It's only going to take a second," Real said, turning the Lambo around and heading back up to the club.

"Man, come on, now! What the hell you hire this nigga for? To watch pussy! Shit, you might as well be managing your own shit! Every night, you get a call to go do his fuckin' job! You need to hire somebody to handle your business so you'll have time to spend with your fuckin' lady!" Constance barked as they pulled up into the club parking lot.

Real knew when it was good to let Constance have her say, especially when she was right, but by the same token, Constance also knew when to hold her tongue.

"Come on," Real told Constance as he opened the door on the Lambo.

Ignoring his command, Constance sat in the car until he walked around, opened up her door, and helped her out of the car. Walking hand in hand, they entered G-Spot.

Chapter 2

" ey, cuz! Two slick-dressed Italian guys demanded to see you. For what, I don't know, but they up in VIP with some of their other friends," Max told Real as he pointed toward the VIP section of the club.

"Italians?" Real repeated, trying to figure out what the men could possibly want. Real didn't know any local Italians.

"Yeah," Max said, looking in their direction.

"What they want?" Constance asked angrily, furious that her night was put on hold by Max—again.

While Constance and Real stood in the middle of the club floor, naked girls spoke to Real and ignored Constance as they walked by. Constance made it known to every girl working that she wouldn't hesitate to fuck them up when it came to Real. Some of the girls respected her situation, but a good majority of them didn't. Every chance one of them got, they would come on to Real in some kind of way. After a while, it was known around the club that Real wasn't going to cheat on Constance, so they stopped trying—all but Cream, the beautiful half-Black, half-White stallion. Cream was determined to break Real down and get him into her bed.

"I told you I don't know what they want," Max snapped

looking at Constance with pure hatred.

"So you called us all the way down here, and you don't even know what they want? Did you even ask?" Constance snapped back.

"I called Real down here, not you," Max answered harshly.

"Enough!" Real yelled, leaving Max and Constance standing in the middle of the floor looking at each other as he went to the VIP section to see what the Italians wanted. "Somebody looking for me?" Real asked, looking at the men.

They instantly stopped throwing money at the naked girl and looked up at him. "Who are you?" asked one of the men.

"I'm Real, the owner. Now, who wants to see me?' Real asked again.

"Oh! Real! Come take a seat, my friend," the young, fancy-dressed Italian told Real after making his friend move out of the seat beside him.

"I'm good. What's the problem?" Real asked, still standing staring the man down.

"Oh, there's no problem, my friend. I just came to deliver a very important message from Mr. Rossi," the young Italian said as he stood and walked over to Real.

"Rossi? What's the message?" Real asked, confused. He didn't recognize the name.

The Italian man got up close on Real and whispered, "Mr. Rossi says you work for him or you don't work at all. He knows you are making his competition, the Moretti family, very rich, which is also making Moretti's stronghold on the cartel a lot stronger. Mr. Rossi can't touch Mr. Moretti at this time, but he can touch you. So, what'll it be?" the young Italian asked with a sly smile.

Real placed his arm around the man's shoulder and said firmly, "Tell your boss Mr. Rossi that I said to go fuck himself and that I don't sit well with threats. Now, you and your boys get the fuck up out of my establishment!" Real said, smiling as he exited the VIP section, motioning for Max and Constance to follow.

"What up, cuz?" Max asked as they entered Real's back office.

"Everything's good. Just some rich, arrogant Italians trying to invest in the club, which is totally out of the question," Real told Max as Constance stood by, picking up on the lie.

"Oh, okay, cuz. I got everything under control. I will call you tomorrow with an update on thangs," Max said, wiping the sweat from his forehead with the back of his hand.

Constance rolled her eyes.

"A'ight, cool," Real said, turning to walk out the office.

"Under control my ass!" Constance uttered as she followed Real out of the back office.

As Real walked across the floor, he noticed the Italians exiting. The tall, lanky one looked in his direction and smiled. Real smiled back.

A few minutes later, Real and Constance were turning out of the G-Spot onto Peachtree Street.

Picking up on Real's different mood, Constance spoke softly. "What's going on, baby?" she asked, sensing his uneasiness.

"Some spic trying to make demands. Had the nerve to send me a message that if I don't work for him, I don't work at all. Can you believe that? Ain't that some shit? He must don't know who the fuck Real is!" Real shouted, getting madder and madder as he thought about the threat from the man in the silky suit.

"Who sent the message?" Constance inquired, trying to see if she recognized the name as one of her wealthy real estate clients. She had sold several high-end homes to Italian drug lords.

"Rossi!" Real spat.

"Hmm. Never heard that name before. So what's next?"

Constance asked.

"I'm going to call old man Moretti to see what the deal is. If he don't fix it, I will!" Real snapped.

"He'll straighten it out," Constance said, hoping he would—but even if he didn't, she was going to ride with Real to the very end, no matter what.

"Look, baby, I really ain't in the mood right now for the play. I really need to make some calls," Real said, knowing that she would understand.

"Okay. Me neither," Constance agreed.

Turning around, Real took the Lambo to speeds it had never reached before on the way back home.

Enjoy a bonus read

from

Visit www.gstreetchronicles.com
to view all our titles

Join us on Facebook
G Street Chronicles Fan Page

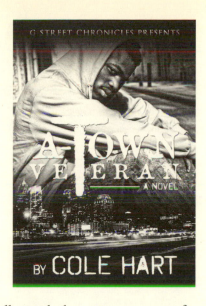

Young Hollywood, the youngest goon of a notorious rich clique from Hollywood Court projects is destined to make his name known throughout the entire Westside of Atlanta. Certified and ruthless, Young Hollywood is worth a half a million before the age of sixteen, and is well on his way until tragedy strikes. Young Hollywood's home is invaded, and his son is held for ransom. Violated, blood thirsty and reckless, he vows for revenge as he combs the city for answers.

Once inside the Georgia Penal System, Young Hollywood continues on his ruthless traits until he is placed on high max with hardened criminals. There, Young Hollywood meets up with a man he never knew before. After they untie, the real A-Town Veteran is released from prison after serving twenty straight years, but not before sucking up every piece of game and knowledge he could.

This entertaining triumph goes from the streets, to the prison system and to the corporate world of record labels and rap entertainment. This highly anticipated, descriptive urban novel about crime, corruption and passion in Atlanta's own underworld will have you on your toes from the first page to the very last. This is one masterpiece you'll never want to end.

A-TOWN VETERAN

THE PLATINUM EDITION

CHAPTER 1

The Fulton County Juvenile Courtroom was crawling with people: screaming children and some of the most nagging old women who would make your skin crawl. Just yap…yap… yap, all about nothing. Even though a lot of them were there to support their kids and grandkids, many of them were there to make sure justice was served against Terry Keys, the notorious thirteen-year-old alleged murderer who was beginning to make his name known throughout the Westside of Atlanta.

In a gun battle with a twenty-one-year-old, Terry Keys didn't hesitate to shoot. He was well trained by the older brothers. If you let the public tell it, the murder was drug related. It had become major news all over the city of Atlanta. Terry Keys had a young, handsome face—the schoolboy type, very innocent looking. His body frame was small and chiseled. His eyebrows were thick and dark, and he wore his hair neatly trimmed in a three-inch afro with not a hair out of place. He was dressed in a navy blue, two-piece suit, a white Polo dress shirt, and a blue tie.

Next to Terry sat his high-priced attorney, well known throughout the city. Andre Rizzi was a slick talker and casual dresser, with a reputation that spoke for itself. It was rumored he was connected with every major drug dealer, armed robber, and hit man in the city. He was known for playing golf, fishing, and eating at the most expensive restaurants with every judge and politician around Atlanta. His name alone carried more weight than a triple-beam scale.

As the proceedings started, the bailiff, a heavyset man in his mid fifties shouted, "All rise!" His voice boomed through the entire courtroom.

Everybody shuffled to their feet. As the judge climbed the steps that led to his bench, Terry Key's heart began erupting inside his chest at just the thought of knowing court was about to start. Terry allowed his eyes to follow the judge, darting with every step.

The judge was a chubby-faced white man, clean-shaven, with salt-and-pepper hair. Clad in his black robe, his suspicious blue eyes searched the courtroom. It was evident that he wanted to make sure everyone was on their feet. "You may be seated," he said. He cleared his throat and adjusted the microphone. He slowly lifted the wire-framed eyeglasses hanging around his neck and slid them on his face. His vision enhanced within a microsecond, and he pretended to be looking over some papers. It was all bullshit, though, and a mask came over his face; all this was just an act. He already knew the case, and he'd already received eight grand from the Regal & Alexander Law Firm as an early Christmas gift.

Andre Rizzi was married to the daughter of the founder of the law firm. Not to mention, Rizzi's wife was the judge's goddaughter. It was all an inside circle—Atlanta's own political secret society. This was something bigger going on than Terry Keys, and it would be years before he would be aware of the game of life; another pawn being moved around the board with the touch of a finger.

The judge finally lifted his head and allowed his eyes to focus directly on Terry Keys. "Young man, are your parents here this morning?" he asked.

There was a short silence. The fact of the matter was that Terry Keys had accepted the streets. His neighborhood, Hollywood Court, was his version of parents. His real biological mother was out there somewhere. Where? He didn't know...and actually, he didn't care. His father couldn't make it to court either. Terry's dad was thirteen years into a double life sentence for two bodies he'd caught in 1980. Terry hadn't ever seen him in person, but he'd heard some hood legends about him; enough to convince him that he got his gangsta from his daddy. It was inherited.

A middle-aged woman on the congested third pew stood up. Her hand slightly raised and fell back to her side just as quick. "I'm his grandmamma," she said. Then she added, "He stay wit' me."

The judge's eyes went to her quickly, and then he motioned his hand for the woman to come to the front of the courtroom. She went and stood before him.

When the judge motioned for Terry to come and stand next to her, he did as he was told and tried desperately hard to keep his mouth closed as much as possible; he didn't want the judge to see his gold teeth. He pressed his lips together and put on the saddest face he could muster.

"Son do you know with a crime like this, you could go to prison for the rest of your life?" the judge asked.

Terry nodded his head and in a clear whisper said, "Yes, sir." His hands and arms were pressed against his sides as if he were in the military.

"Is that what you want?" the judge asked.

"No, sir," Terry responded.

The judge looked at Terry's grandmother. Her skin was mahogany, and there were thin bags under her eyes. Her hair was made up in thick finger waves. She wore a red turtleneck sweater, white jeans, and boots. A diamond rope chain hung loosely around her neck. She stared into the judge's eyes, and he offered her the same stare. "What is your name?" he asked.

"Vickie Keys," she said.

"Miss Keys, where are you currently living right now?" asked the judge.

"Hollywood Court on Hollywood Road," she said proudly. Her eyes gleamed, and she stood even more erect and raised her head.

The judge curled his lips as if he were really impressed and began nodding his rather large head. He couldn't really respond because if he did, he wouldn't have anything positive to say about Westside Atlanta. It was 1991. The murder rate was at an all-time high, and the crack era was in full effect. The judge took a sip of water from the glass that sat to the right of him. He glanced around the courtroom again and noticed how impatient and agitated everyone looked. Sharply, his eyes cut back to Terry Keys. He asked, "Are you attending school?"

"Yes, sir," Terry responded. "I go to Usher Middle School." As he swallowed, his Adam's apple bobbled in his throat; he'd just told a straight-faced lie.

The judge picked up a fountain pen and pointed it toward Terry and narrowed his eyes. "You are still a child, son. I don't want to hear your name, nor do I want to see you in my courtroom ever again. You need to stay your tail in school and get yourself an education," the judge said. It was the quickest type of lecture that came to his head. He looked to the grandmother. "I'm giving him three years of probation with a monthly report from you."

She nodded, and a bright smile appeared across her face. She dropped her arm around her grandson's neck and pulled him to her.

The judge hit his gavel. "Next case on the docket!" he yelled.

Terry Keys and his grandmother turned and headed toward the defense table, where Andre Rizzi gave them a smile and extended his hand. Vickie shook his hand first, and Terry followed. Andre Rizzi held on to Terry's small boy hand and said, "Good luck and tell Wayne everything went well and to give me a call in the morning."

Terry Keys nodded and gave the attorney one final shake before they departed. He and his grandmother moved swiftly up the aisle and exited the courtroom. But in the midst of the many people and families, there still lurked anger and bitter feelings about the outcome. And if anyone wanted revenge, they would also be looking for war.

Other titles from

G STREET CHRONICLES

City Lights
A-Town Veteran
Executive Mistress
Essence of a Bad Girl
Two Face
Dealt the Wrong Hand
Dope, Death & Deception
Family Ties
Blocked In
Drama

The Love, Lust & Lies Series by Mz. Robinson
Married to His Lies
What We Won't Do for Love

"Coming Fall 2011"
The Lies We Tell for Love
(part 3 of Mz. Robinson's Love, Lust & Lies Series)

Still Deceiving
(part 2 of India's Dope, Death & Deception)

"Coming 2012"
Trap House
Drama II

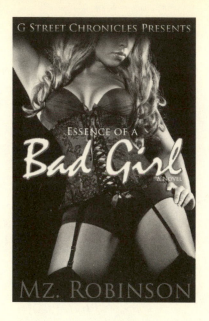

Essence Monroe went through great lengths to escape her sordid past and the lovers in it. Using extreme and deadly tactics she re-invented herself and now she's well on her way to a promising future. Not only is she engaged to Andrew Carlton, one of Atlanta's most sought after athletes, but she's slowly creating a name for herself in the fashion industry. Essence is a former bad girl—gone good and she's living a life that others can only dream of. That is until Essence's life is shaken, when she discovers that someone knows her secrets. When threats turn into blackmail, Essence must revert to her bad girl ways. While she's focused on keeping her skeletons buried, there's another woman focused on taking her place by Andrew's side. Not only does the mysterious woman want to take Essence's man but she wants Essence life for her very own.

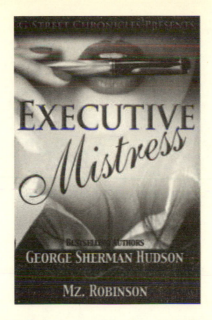

G&L Enterprises is the biggest marketing firm in the country. Each year thousands of intern applicants apply with the hope of securing a position with the illustrious firm. Out of a sea of applicants, Asia is bestowed the honor of receiving an internship with G&L. Asia is beautiful, ambitious, and determined to climb her way up the corporate ladder by any means necessary. From crossing out all in her path, to seducing Parker Bryant the CEO of G&L, Asia secures a permanent position with the marketing giant. However, her passion for success will not allow her to settle for second best. Asia wants the number one spot, and she'll stop at nothing, including betraying the man responsible for her success to get it. Asia, is taking corporate takeover to a whole new level!

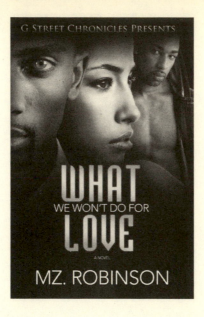

Octavia Ellis is a sexy and independent woman who plays it safe when it comes down to relationships. She lives by one rule: keep it strictly sexual. Octavia is living her life just the way she wants. No man. No issues. No drama. When she meets the handsome Damon Whitmore, everything changes. Octavia soon finds that Damon has become a part of her world and her heart. However, when temptation comes in the form of a sexy-hardcore thug named, Beau, Octavia finds herself caught in a deadly love triangle. She soon learns in life and love, there are no rules and she's surprised at what she herself, will not do for love.

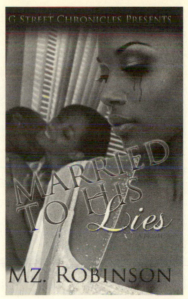

Shontay Holloway is as faithful as they come when it comes to her husband, Kenny. For eight years she's been his support system physically and financially. She's managed to overlook the fact that he's a woman chaser and even turned the other cheek when he got another woman pregnant. Shontay would rather work it out with Kenny than start fresh with someone new. She's not satisfied but she is content. Is there really a difference? Shontay doesn't think so, but that soon changes when she meets Savoy Breedwell.

Shontay finds herself torn between her vows and the man she's falling for. When tragedy strikes, Shontay learns that the love she thought her husband had for her is nothing more than a cover up for his true intentions. She becomes a woman on a mission. When she's finished, Till death do us part, may have a whole new meaning.

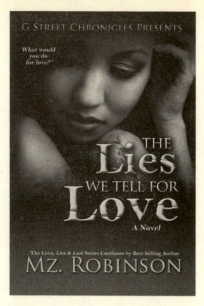

Coming October 2011

"What would you do for love?"
"How would you handle the discovery that your marriage was built on lies?"

As the drama unfolds, lies and secrets will be exposed and lines will be crossed on both ends. How far will Damon and Octavia go to protect each other from the other's transgressions and how many will fall victim to the lies that have been spun in the name of love?

Keshawn Flower, also known as KeKe, is an 8 year old girl who was taken in by her grandparents. Though Compton, Ca. was where she resided the household and neighborhood in which she lived was far from ghetto. As a matter of fact it was close to perfection.

KeKe gets hit with devastating news and finds herself being forced to embrace the street life and take care of herself. Gang banging, dope selling, and numerous robberies are the highlights of her new life. It was go hard or go home and unfortunately there was no home.

The demon inside KeKe had turned into the Incredible Hulk. She flips the city upside down killing everything in sight. Rage is her new best friend and the streets are learning first hand what KeKe brings to the game.

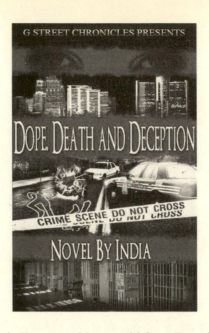

Meet Lovely Brown, a 20 year old from Detroit, MI that has witnessed too much! After her father was sentenced to major time behind bars her mother turns to drugs and is later found dead because of it. She is left to take care of her younger sister after her older sister bails! She's been homeless and hungry, taking various street jobs to put food on the table for her baby sister Tori, but after a case of mistaken identity Lovely is left all alone with no family because they've all become victims of the streets, in one way or another. She vows to take vengeance into her own hands and shut down the dope game by becoming one of it's major players, operating under the name LB. Everything was running smoothly until she finds out that she has a 1 MILLION dollar bounty placed on her head and seemingly overnight everything begins to fall apart. In the mist of her chaos she falls in love with a guy that she knows little about. They've both been keeping secrets but his could prove to be deadly for her! Immediately she thinks of an exit strategy but will she make it out the game alive?

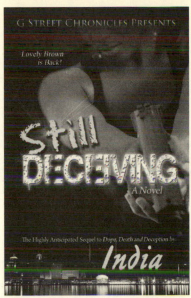

G STREET CHRONICLES PRESENTS

Lovely Brown is Back!

Still DECEIVING

A Novel

The Highly Anticipated Sequel to *Dope, Death and Deception* by:

India

Highly Anticipated Sequel to
Dope Death and Deception

Lovely Brown was living the good life as Detroit's top drug dealer, operating under the alias LB. Everything was going smooth until her father Lucifer escaped from prison, ready to return to the throne and destroy anyone in his path, including Lovely. While running for her life, she was also being investigated by the Feds and simultaneously set-up for the murder of her mafia connects' nephew. This resulted in a ONE MILLION DOLLAR bounty being placed on her head. Achieving the impossible, Lovely managed to escape unscathed.

Now, five years after she left all the Dope, Death and Deception behind and she's finally living a normal life, things get complicated. Issues from her past come right to her front door. Once again Lovely finds herself in a bad situation with her back against the wall—looking sideways at everyone in her corner. Lies have been told and love has been tested.

Just when she thought things were over, it looks as if someone is Still Deceiving!

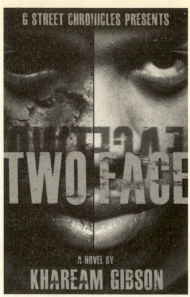

Trapped in time, Jay is a prisoner of his own mind. A victim of multiple personalities, Jay and his alter ego Capo are two very different men sharing one body. Jay is a laid back man who has grown tired of the streets and doing his cousin Ant's dirty work. Although, those close to Jay have grown to love and accept both of his personalities, he longs to gain control and walk away from the murder and madness his other half is creating. Capo is a possessed killing machine, who thrives on shedding the blood of others. Death is his counselor and killing is his therapy, he spares no opportunity to take a life. Taral is a slave for Capo. Whatever he desires is her command. Struggling with her own demons, Taral is a crazed nympho seeking the attention from anyone who will have her. On the other side there is Charlene, Jay's wife. After seeing her husband being beat and dragged she went into a state of depression, not knowing that her curiosity sparked her husband's brutal attack. Follow these characters from the dirtiest and deadliest streets in Atlanta to the city's most patronized strip clubs. The lies, deceit and mayhem moves from coast to coast as the mystery behind Two Face and the sins of these four individuals unfold.

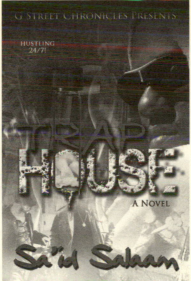

Trap House is an unflinching account of the goings on of an Atlanta drug den and the lives of those who frequent it. Its cast of characters include the Notorious P.I.G., the proprietor of the house, who uses his power to satisfy his licentious fetishes. Of his customers, there's Wanda, an exotic dancer who loathes P.I.G., but only tolerates him because he has the best dope in town. Wanda's boyfriend Mike is the owner of an upscale strip club, as well as a full time pimp.

Tiffany and Marcus are the teenage couple who began frequenting the Trap House after snorting a few lines at a party. Can their love for each other withstand the demands of their fledging addiction, or will it tear them apart?

P.I.G.'s wife Blast, doorman Earl and a host of other colorful characters round out the inhabitants of the Trap House.

Trap House is the bastard child of real life and the author's vivid imagination. Its author, Sa'id Salaam, paints a graphic portrait of the inner-workings of an under-world. He takes you so close you can almost hear the sizzle of the cocaine as it's smoked—almost smell the putrid aroma of crack as it's exhaled. Yet for all the grit and grime, Trap House has the audacity to be a love story. Through the sordid sex and brutality is an underlying tale of redemption and self empowerment. Trap House drives home the reality that everyone is a slave to something.

Who's your master?

Name: _____

Address: _____

City/State: _____

Zip: _____

ALL BOOKS ARE $10 EACH

QTY	TITLE	PRICE
	Beastmode	
	City Lights	
	A-Town Veteran	
	Executive Mistress	
	Essence of a Bad Girl	
	Dope, Death and Deception	
	Dealt the Wrong Hand	
	Married to His Lies	
	What We Won't Do for Love	
	Two Face	
	Family Ties	
	Blocked In	
	Drama	
	Shipping & Handling ($4 1st book/$2 ea additional)	

TOTAL $ _____

To order online visit
www.gstreetchronicles.com
Send cashiers check or money order to:
G Street Chronicles
P.O. Box 490082 College Park, GA 30349